Thomas Russell Sullivan

Day and Night Stories

Thomas Russell Sullivan

Day and Night Stories

ISBN/EAN: 9783744747363

Printed in Europe, USA, Canada, Australia, Japan

Cover: Foto ©Andreas Hilbeck / pixelio.de

More available books at **www.hansebooks.com**

DAY AND NIGHT STORIES.

DAY AND NIGHT STORIES

BY

T. R. SULLIVAN

HORATIO. — O day and night, but this is wondrous strange!
HAMLET. — And therefore as a stranger give it welcome.

NEW YORK
CHARLES SCRIBNER'S SONS
1890

University Press
JOHN WILSON AND SON, CAMBRIDGE

TO THE MEMORY OF

𝔐𝔶 𝔅𝔯𝔬𝔱𝔥𝔢𝔯,

HENRY DORR SULLIVAN.

CONTENTS.

DAY AND NIGHT STORIES.

THE LOST REMBRANDT.

I have been half in love with easeful Death.
Ode to a Nightingale.

THE lovely old city of The Hague, now, as always, withdrawn from the vulgarizing influences of commerce, has an indescribable air of refinement, much dwelt upon in the books and peculiarly its own. This is due, as any writer of guides will bear me out in saying, to the fact that the town grew up around the royal hunting-box, and has been, since Holland was, the favorite resort of Dutch princes. And the same writer will probably go on to tell you that by leaving your hotel at six A. M., you can in one day see it all, — *all*, even to its flippant watering-place, two miles off, among the dunes on the melancholy shore of the North Sea. And so, with this impression of dulness setting as it were the seal upon his own, he will cheerfully whirl you away to view the Leyden University and the Haarlem tulips, with no

1

effort whatsoever, from the window of your railway carriage.

But if you are of a certain age, and temperate; if time has touched you gently, inclining you to be sad and civil, like Malvolio; if you are fond of the light that falls aslant into old pictures; and if, above all, the commercial spirit of your own enterprising nation often oppresses and disheartens you, — why, then you will walk leisurely back from Scheveningen over the ancient dike, that is really a long, straight, lofty arbor of interlacing elm-branches; and you will wonder at the contentment in the faces of the peasant women, and at the barbaric gilded crowns and ear-rings which they wear. On either hand you will catch glimpses of sunny gardens, and choose more than one villa you would be glad to call your own; while the trees go on before you, in among the broad canals and splendid city squares, where all the houses seem palaces, built for comfort, with no state apartments in them, until a few steps more have brought you to the border of the shadowy wood, upon which the old hunting-seat now encroaches. Here are acres of superb beeches, with mossy trunks and gnarled roots, recalling some enchanted forest of the brothers Grimm, and that picture of it left over in your memory from the pantomime of childhood; only now you find the dreadful abode of fabulous monsters and misshapen goblins haunted merely by an invisible chorus of blackbirds, too far above your head to fear or even to heed you. Who calls that place dull where town and country meet upon such terms? Forgive the Dutchmen, for the moment, if they take their pleasures somewhat sadly, as the English do. It is true that the city's one poor theatre is closed in this warm June weather. But the train is always panting to take you back to Paris : stay here a little longer, if only for a day or two.

The Hague has its open jewel-casket, and therein its captain-jewel. When you make your first visit to Maurice of Nassau's house, now transformed into a museum, you will pass through certain anterooms, where the two wives of Rubens, his father-confessor, a glorious Faun and Nymph of Jordaens, and a likeness of William of Orange, by some unknown but strong and tender hand, will all delight you. Then, at the top of the great staircase you will hesitate for a moment, as one often does in all the galleries, wondering which way to turn. A look to the left will decide the question. There is the load-star ; no other guide is needed. You stand a long time before it, and turn away only to come back. You are surrounded by fine pictures, half of them to be forgotten within the next hour ; but this one you will remember through all the after years.

It is the " Lesson in Anatomy " of Rembrandt. A famous surgeon is explaining to five brothers of his guild the muscles in the arm of a subject upon the dissecting-table. And not to these eager listen-

ers alone are the words and gesture of the man
directed ; for he stands in a vaulted hall, and looks
beyond you to the imaginary audience, of which,
losing your own identity, you for the time being
form a part. All the world knows this masterpiece from countless reproductions ; but only those
who have seen the picture can fully understand the
charm in the painter's noble treatment of it that
compels one to overlook its disagreeable motive.

The light streams down upon the dead man ; yet
you hardly know he is there. It is death, indeed,
and painted so truthfully that to shut out the living faces is to shudder at it. Bring them back,
and this central object which so fixes their attention has no power upon yours. They glow with
color, they breathe ; you are ready to swear that
one has moved a little. Hark ! the lecturer has
spoken. Alas! his voice has been hushed for
more than two centuries. All these that look
have become even as the thing they look at ; their
very dust is now unrecognizable. And while the
beauty of this life completely fills your thought,
all life's sadness, all the mystery of death, lie on
the canvas there before you.

One day, on my way out of the gallery, I turned
back for another look at the Rembrandt. The
noon light was superb, and there was no one about ;
so I stayed on, absorbed in the picture, and studying it from every possible point of view. At last,
determined to go, I made some commonplace excla-

mation of delight or regret, speaking aloud, as when alone one may without undue absence of mind. A slight movement behind me brought me to myself, and looking over my shoulder I saw that I had been overheard by a little gray, old man, who had come quietly into the room by another door. He was plainly dressed, closely shaven, and his somewhat heavy features had nothing distinctive about them; yet I felt sure that I had seen him before. But one often has this fancy, and I dismissed it at once, even though I had caught him in the act of eying me curiously; for I saw at a glance that he was a Dutchman, and my acquaintance in Holland was limited to landlords and bankers, with an occasional porter or two. The man turned from me to the Rembrandt almost immediately, and I could only be provoked with myself for my small display of emotion. This had amused him, naturally. I must be more self-contained in future. With these mental notes I went away.

But the next day and the day after I found him there again. Then, to avoid him, I changed the hour of my daily visit; to no purpose. Whenever I went to the gallery, this strange companion was sure to make his appearance before I left it. I tried not to notice him, and sometimes he hardly noticed me; but once or twice I could not help observing that he seemed pleased when we met, as usual, in the Rembrandt room. He never spoke, never saluted me, never sought in any way to make

his presence an intrusion. He irritated me, nevertheless. I could no more see my favorite picture
apart from this gray shadow than I could stand in
the sunlight and escape my own.

I pointed him out to each of the custodians in
turn. They all agreed in recognizing him as a
familiar creature, but none knew his name. If I
expressed surprise, or questioned further, I was ·
either politely referred to the visitors' book, — that
labyrinth without a clew, — or I was given, in imperfect English, a summary of the custodial duties,
of which a personal acquaintance with all mankind
had never been reckoned one. He did no injury ;
he molested nobody. Upon these conditions the
gallery was open to him. What would I have ?

What, indeed ? I could complain of nothing ;
the annoyance was of my own making. Why
should this man dog my steps with no apparent
purpose ? Could it be a case of mistaken identity ?
Was I, through a chance resemblance, in danger
of arrest for some extraordinary crime ? No. Were
I really shadowed, in that sense of the word, I
should be the last to know it. Besides, I had become convinced that my first impression was cor-
rect, and that I had of the man some knowledge
earlier than any I could now recall. Moreover, he
emphasized himself, so to speak, by never leaving
the gallery before me. Once I waited in a remote
corner until the hour of closing, with the conviction that this time he would be forced to take the

lead. When I ventured out it was to find him standing, with the rigid patience of a lackey, near the head of the staircase. At the sight of me he drew back with a courteous gesture that was almost servile. Further persistence on my part would involve conversation, perhaps fellowship. I accepted the situation, and went first, lifting my hat formally. At the door I looked back and saw him slowly following; but I had already passed out of his thoughts, and my look was not returned.

I might have played the shadow in my turn, and watching my chance, have dogged him to his own door. But this scheme, I argued, if detected, would lead me into endless complication; if carried out successfully, it could avail me little, — I might learn his address, his occupation, perhaps his name, for all which, as I persuaded myself, I cared next to nothing. I wanted to ignore him, to forget him; but I was not long permitted to do either.

One evening after dinner I strolled lazily away from the hotel-porch to smoke my cigar in the gathering twilight upon the shore of the Vyver. This pretty sheet of water lies in the centre of all things, and has, to mark its own central point, a little mossy island, around which many garrulous ducks and stately swans go always gliding, — as if they bore in those unruffled breasts vague longings vaster than their appetites, and less likely to be satisfied. On one side the irregular, mediæval Palace of the Binnenhof springs directly from the

water, and throws back upon the waveless surface
a reflection that seems to sink deeper than its own
foundations. There are strange gate-ways and
high-pitched roofs and oddly ornamented towers;
while, farther off, the great Church of St. Jacob
thrusts itself up from the humming market-place;
and opposite the palace, a broad, shady walk runs
the whole length of the Vyver, with now and then
a seat, where a man may take his ease and watch
all this, and let the great world hum on in the distance. And if he remembers that he is a little
lonely, just a very little, when the stars come out,
and the recesses of the Binnenhof grow deep
and black under his eyes, why then that tinge of
loneliness suits the place and helps it, so long
as the pain does not prove acute enough to be
unbearable.

Upon this memorable evening I found the Vyver-
berg crowded with good city folk, walking sedately
up and down under the trees. They looked so dull
that, thankful for not knowing them, I turned back
to the ducks and muttered Voltaire's malicious
marginal note upon his life in Holland, " Canaux,
canards, canaille ! " Here was his picture, repro-
ducing itself in little, to perfection. Then the light
waned, and the throng gradually dispersed; until,
at the end of my second cigar, I was left almost
alone. I smoked on, trying to lose myself in my
thoughts. But night came down with a rush, for
there was no moon; and it brought up my wander-

ing senses more than once with a round turn. The stars grew brilliant, and the lamps cast sharp lines of light into the water. It was picturesque, but disagreeably damp and chilly too. I shivered a little; then I thought of the homely saying that a man shivers when a step has been taken somewhere, a long way off, upon the spot of earth destined for his grave; and at this not over-cheerful suggestion I shivered again. "I shall catch my death," I mentally predicted. The cigar was bitter; I tossed it away, and got up to go.

As I turned out into the path I saw a man moving slowly toward me in the darkness on the very edge of the basin. At the first glimpse of his figure two thoughts came to me like successive lightning flashes, — that I had never encountered my tormenting shadow in the open air, and that this was he. I stood still. The light from one of the street-lamps must have fallen upon my face; for as the man came nearer, he looked up, saw me, and starting a little, lost his balance and stepped back into the water of the Vyver.

I knew that it was very shallow; but of course I dashed forward and helped him out. He had fallen flat, and I found him thoroughly limp and wet. He shivered, and his hands were cold. To my surprise he thanked me in good English, speaking very simply; and his voice was decidedly agreeable. He did not laugh or even smile at his accident; yet he treated it lightly, and his way of taking it made me forget its ludicrous side.

" I will find you a carriage," I said.

" Oh, no ; I should walk, it is better. I am cold."

" But not alone. That will not do."

And thereupon, forgetting my former antipathy, I pulled out my card and actually offered to walk home with him.

He looked at the card and read the name, as we stood there under the lamp.

" Yes," he said, " you are at the Marshal Turenne. I have no card about me ; but I am called Lucas Grafman. You are very kind. I could go alone, yet I shall be glad of your company. Will you walk on ? It is cold."

It did not strike me as strange that he should know the name of my hotel. I felt that we were in sympathy, and I was anxious to learn more of him ; yet I hesitated to put leading questions. We walked for some time in silence and at a slow pace, his gait being uncertain and feeble ; until, as we turned a corner, and came out into the great square of the Plein, one side of which was ablaze with lighted windows, he stopped and sighed.

" You are tired," I said.

He shook his head, and avoiding the shops, led the way across the darkest part of the square, by the statue of William the Silent, and so on under the trees.

" Where have we met before?" I asked abruptly.

He pointed at the dark Mauritshuis, just definable through the wavering shadows.

" There, — in the Rembrandt room," he answered.

" Yes; but before that."

" Never before that." Then quickening his pace, he added, " A little faster; I am cold."

It made me cold myself to walk beside him. But his voice was low and sweet as the night-murmur of a brook. I liked to hear it.

" Do we go much farther ? " I asked again.

" No, only a little, — a very little." He went on as if he were talking to himself. " The way is short, and it is sure. No one can miss it." ˙

We crossed the top of the Spui, where all the bustle and movement evidently distressed him. Another turn into a narrow, dimly lighted street put him at his ease. He looked at me, saying almost gayly, —

" You do not regret your kindness ? I have not bored you ? "

" No; on the contrary."

" Good! I thank you."

The street brought us out upon the brink of a sluggish canal, which we followed for a few steps under a row of dark houses, all leaning different ways, with the uncanny effect peculiar to old buildings in that sea-disputed land. These looked as though one touch would send them tottering to their fall. Halfway down the row he stopped.

" This is the door."

He went up to it, and pulled a bell that rang in the distance, echoing back to us as if through deserted rooms. After a moment's delay he called, but so faintly that even I scarcely heard him, —

" Yanna! Adriana!"

There was no answer. He groped about, apparently for a key, which he must have found. I could hear the grating of the lock. Then, as he held the door half open, I had a glimpse of the hall, where a dying lamp was on the point of giving up the ghost of its flame.

" Will you come in ?" he asked.

I excused myself. The hour was late.

" But you will come again ?"

Why should I ? I hesitated. All my old dislike to him returned.

A sound decided me, — the sound of low, sweet music in the house. There was a woman singing. I could not distinguish the words, but I knew that the voice was a young girl's.

" Yanna! Adriana!" he called softly as before ; and there was no more singing.

" You will come again ?" he repeated.

" Yes."

" To-morrow, then ; at this hour. I shall expect you."

And he was gone. The door fell back behind him. The place was horribly still. There was no sign of life, no movement, except in the mist slowly streaming up from the canal to fold itself about me like a winding-sheet. I lost no time in getting clear of it.

The next morning though I paid my usual visit to the gallery it was not to see the pictures. Even upon the great Rembrandt I turned my back, and went from room to room with but one thought, — that of meeting Mynheer Grafman. All in vain. He was not there, and his unwonted absence set me thinking. Was he ill? That might well be, considering his accident of the night before. In the broad daylight I had gone more than halfway toward a resolve to break my reluctant word with him. What possible good can come of our appointment I had asked myself, after sleeping upon it soundly. But now I felt in duty bound to keep the promise, if only to prove that I had startled him unwittingly, to show a decent regret for his false step in the dark, of which, innocently, I had been the cause.

Yet I found more than one misgiving left to conquer when the time came. A lonely walk after dark, in a strange city, at best is not alluring. And afterward? What risk might I not run in crossing that dismal threshold? If the old man were a decoy, the house a den of thieves? I laughed these thoughts away. My watch weighed so little, and I carried nothing else of value; my money, in a letter of credit, to a thief would be

unavailable. I was in for an adventure, mildly interesting, perhaps; but what were travel without
adventures? Nevertheless, I gave the hotel-cham-
ber that mute farewell one bids his household gods
on the eve of a long journey. With this too went
certain precautions. I left upon the dressing-table
a line to indicate my destination, so far as I knew
it; I closed the door of my room without turning
the key; and finding below the monumental *portier*,
resplendent in steel buttons and silver lace, I passed
the time of night with him, taking pains to state
the precise hour of my return. He twirled the
waxed ends of his absurdly small moustache, then
smiled and nodded confidentially. His keen glance
was my best assurance. The soul of the Marshal
Turenne would not fail to be disquieted, in case my
absence were prolonged.

I followed the narrow street to the pale mists of
the canal. This was the place, and there the house
I wanted, — the fifth from the corner, I remembered that. I pulled the bell, which jangled again
remotely with the sound I knew, and immediately
the door was opened by a tall, white-haired man-
servant in dark livery.

"Mynheer Grafman?"

He bowed and moved aside to let me pass, then
led the way into the long hall, painted white and
panelled, with here and there a portrait frowning
down. At the farther end I saw a staircase in its
carved spiral of balustrade. But he stopped half-

way, and, lifting a piece of faded tapestry, waited silently for me to go in. I did so, and felt the curtain fall heavily into its place.

I seemed to step at once into the golden age of Holland. The high walls of the huge drawing-room were hung with splendid pictures that out-shone the gilding of their heavy frames. The polished furniture was carved into strange shapes and richly ornamented. There were odd, rococo cabinets, revealing through their glass doors many precious objects, — gold and silver drinking-cups, ancient prizes of the hunting-feast, South Sea curios of coral, ivory, and jade. The soft Eastern carpets and softer hangings had those subdued tints that only time's slowly moving shuttle weaves; the crystal drops of the sconces glowed with candle-light; and upon the wide hearth, in spite of the season, a fire had been kindled. In the chimney-corner stood a harp, and close beside it, on a heap of crumpled music, a jar of yellow roses. Their perfume, strengthened by the warmth of the fire, filled the room. Only this handful of flowers held the odor of the present in them; all else belonged to an interior that Terburgh might have painted for background to a knight and lady smiling over a love-letter. And my timid fancy had pictured it a den of thieves!

Mynheer Grafman left his seat by the fire, and came forward to meet me. He did not offer his hand, but greeted me with grave cordiality.

"You are welcome," he said. "I feared you might forget."

His voice had the same clear note, which again disarmed me.

"I could not forget," I answered, "that through me you were caused annoyance, possibly serious. You are none the worse for your accident?"

"No; as you see."

He went back to his place, inviting me with a gesture to draw closer and be seated.

As I turned for a chair, the curtain was brushed aside, and I saw in the doorway the slender figure of a young girl so lovely that I stood still and stared at her in speechless wonder, almost fearing to breathe, lest I should wake from a dream to long for her forever. But she dropped the curtain, and came into the room.

She wore pale yellow, the color of the roses, with no ornament except a white camellia. It could not match the whiteness of her throat; and her arms, bare to the elbow, might have been the missing ones of Melos, they were so delicately rounded. Her hair was black, and its heavy braid fell over one shoulder to her waist. Her eyes were black too; they had no laughter in them; they deepened the sadness of the face, yet it was of beauty indescribable, beyond all other beauty of the earth. I can only liken it to the face of night, just flushed with the rosy tint of morning, — mournful, but submissive; reluctant to go, yet preparing to be gone.

There was an awkward moment of silence before my host looked up and presented me.

"It is my daughter Adriana," he then said tenderly.

She bent her head but did not offer her hand.

"It is not the custom," I thought, wondering in what language to address her.

Then she spoke, in English.

"You are welcome." That was all. But her father's voice seemed harsh after those words.

I stammered incoherent thanks for her kindness to a stranger.

"I knew we were to meet," she answered. "Let us forget that we are strangers."

She turned away, while I sat down, as her father begged me to do. I listened to his talk, thinking only of her, and following her with my eyes. She brought a low table, and set it down between us; then placed upon it two glasses with curiously twisted stems, and after filling these from a silver-mounted flagon, she handed one to me.

"That you may forget," she said gently.

My hand shook a little as I took the glass. The time, the place, and her strange presence, all had something fearful in them. The wine was black, but through it one crimson bubble, glowing like fire, rose to the brim and broke.

"Will you not drink?" said the old man, pausing with his own glass at his lips.

"Friends, always!" I murmured, drinking as I

2

spoke, and looking from him to her, while she whispered back my words.

So, in honor of the toast, we drained the glasses.

" Fill again!" said Mynheer Grafman, as we put them down. The liquor had the richness of an Italian *vino spumante,* or some old Burgundy of noted vintage; but it was very cold, and its fine, aromatic flavor was quite unknown to me.

" What wine is this ? " I asked.

" The grapes were grown in Java," he replied; " and this cask of mine has, in its time, made many voyages. The wine is rare and old, but there is no harm in it."

" None whatever," said I, sipping it again. " These were grapes, indeed." The draught had an effect upon me more than pleasant, wonderfully soothing. I settled myself in ·my chair, and felt at peace with all the world. Care and sorrow seemed to float away in an alembic fume. There was in my past one bitter hour, whose recollection had never failed to move me. I thought of it now indifferently, as though it were another man's; I could not even sigh at it. And of the future I thought nothing. I was there; I saw her; I was content with the present moment, so content as to believe that it would last.

Mynheer Grafman asked me if I liked music.

" Yes," I answered eagerly; " to the music of last night I could listen always."

"Yanna!" he said, looking up at her and dwelling on the affectionate diminutive; "Yanna!"

She had been standing behind his chair, but now she crossed the room, and seating herself at the harp, stretched one white arm across it to try the strings. Of all instruments, the harp is perhaps the one best suited to graceful girlhood; and I found it hard not to startle her into a consciousness of her own beauty with a false note of admiration.

The song was in her native language, and I understood no phrase of it; yet my eyes filled with tears. I could not praise her voice; and though its sweetness lives in my mind's ear like the sea's voice in a shell, I cannot put it into words, — it won my heart. She stopped singing, and played on, till the music, note by note, had died away.

"The song?" I asked. "What is it? What does it mean?"

"It is a song about life," she answered.

"Life!" I repeated. "There was a sob in every word. Can life, then, be so sad a thing?"

"There is nothing in all the universe so sad as human life," she said with perfect calmness, as though this were to her a truth long since established past all disputing.

"No matter!" I cried. "Though it be a wail, I must know your song by heart. Sing it to me again, — once more, I beg of you!"

She hesitated, but her father made a warning gesture. She rose, left the harp, and went directly to the door, as if in obedience to the signal.

"Not now," she said, with her hand already at the curtain. "No more, until we meet again."

"But that may never be," I urged.

"Yes, sooner or later, it will surely be. All rests with you." And she was gone.

I longed to speak of her, but this was not permitted. My host seemed bent upon changing the current of my thoughts. He led me about the room, opening the cabinets to give me a closer look at their contents, talking of them rapidly and of the pictures.

"There is a Hobbema, and here a Ruisdael. This horn is of wrought silver, — good work, it might pass for a Cellini. The other is of later date, inferior, as you see. That portrait is a Rembrandt." I started involuntarily, remembering our first meeting. He stopped for a moment, then went up to the picture.

"It is Nicolaas Tulp," he continued, "the painter's friend and patron. You remember?"

"Perfectly. It is he who gives the 'Lesson in Anatomy.'"

"Yes," he said, turning upon me with an attentive look which was somewhat disconcerting.

"Why does he do that?" I thought; "I will keep a sharp lookout for him in the mirror." Then I noticed for the first time, with wondering eyes, that, in spite of the rich appointments, there was no mirror of any kind in the room.

Meanwhile the other went on, still talking of the once famous surgeon.

"The same man, of course," said he; "without his hat, this time. But you recognize him, do you not? The likeness is unmistakable."

"To be sure," I returned lightly. "Mynheer Tulp and I are old friends. I greet him cordially. This is he, beyond all question."

We looked at the portrait for a time in silence. Then Mynheer Grafman spoke again.

"You are very fond of Rembrandt," said he.

"Yes; and especially of his masterpiece, — the picture in the Mauritshuis, of which we were just now speaking."

"Pardon me; his master-work is not there."

"Oh," I said, "I expressed but my own opinion. The world will tell you of the 'Night-Watch,' so called, in Amsterdam —"

"Pardon me; nor is it there in Amsterdam."

"And where else should one look for it?" I demanded.

"One, indeed!" was his strange answer. "The world has looked long in vain for what one man may see."

"What do you mean?"

"Hush! not so loud. Wait, and I will show you."

He went over to the high chimney-piece and laid

his hand upon one of its smaller panels; with some
slight pressure the bit of wood turned upon a pivot,
disclosing a shallow hiding-place from which he
took a rusty key and an old brass lamp. He pushed
the panel into place again, and lighting the lamp,
looked about uneasily; then beckoned me to
follow.

At the back of the room was a long window,
which he opened stealthily. "Make no noise!"
he whispered, as we stepped out upon the loose
pavement of a terrace encumbered with dusty
vines. We passed down the broken steps and
on through a neglected garden. In its grass-
grown paths the glow-worms were shining faintly;
and, as we walked, the toads leaped right and
left before us into beds of straggling flowers
choked with weeds. Along one side a line of
out-buildings, dark and dingy, stretched away
from the house. Following this almost to the
end, he stopped at a low door and tried his key.
After some effort, with more noise than he cared
to make, it turned in the lock, and we went in.

I stood in a stone chamber, built like a cellar
or a crypt, with a vaulted ceiling. There were
wooden shelves crowded with glass vessels, plump
and unwieldy, some with wicker covers. Rows
of casks loomed up in the darkness; some of
these were empty, some still contained liquor, or
perhaps, were only reeking with its fumes. The
dampness was visible; my breath turned to vapor,

and touching the wall, I felt there a patch of mould.

" It was once a wine-shop," whispered Mynheer Grafman, holding the lamp above his head with one hand and feeling his way forward with the other.

I waited near the door, watching him. As he went on, I began to see that the opposite wall-space was entirely filled by a large picture with figures indistinct, at first, and spectral in the darkness. But my guide stopped under a hanging shelf to light a pair of many-branched candelabra that stood upon it ; and as the flames flashed up I gave, incautiously, loud expression to my wonder and delight. He silenced me with a stern gesture ; and hurrying back, he listened for a moment to the dismal call of the insects in the garden. Then he shut the door and locked it.

" Now we may speak freely," he said ; " but not too loud."

I did not care to speak. My eyes spoke for me. What I saw was a pendant, undoubtedly, to the great Rembrandt of the Hague Museum ; though it looked larger than that in this cramped space. The composition recalled the " Lesson in Anatomy," but differed from it widely in all details. The portraits were of other men in other attitudes. The operating surgeon, uncovered, was older than Mynheer Tulp, with a face far stronger than his and finer. His subject, so foreshortened

that the hands appeared almost to touch the feet,
lay turned directly toward me ; and this partially
draped figure, so like death that it must once
have lived, was the body of a woman. But here
the noble quality of the other picture reasserted
itself. This hideousness, thrust into the fore-
ground, failed to catch the eye. All my admiration went up to the group around it. " Life,
life ! " was my one thought ; " these men were
made to be immortal."

Out of my startled silence I was brought back
to myself by an unpleasant consciousness that
Mynheer Grafman had again been closely watching me. I turned quickly, to detect and to confuse
him ; but he looked away indifferently.

" You were perfectly right," I said ; " this is
Rembrandt's masterpiece."

" Yes," he replied. " The surgeon is the illustrious Johannes Deyman, inspector of the Col-
legium Medicum. For many years the picture
hung in the old Weighing-House at Amsterdam
opposite its companion, the ' Lesson in Anatomy.'
Then — " He stopped and sighed.

" Then ? " I repeated.

" The corporation needed money. They sold
their birthright for a mess of pottage. Offered
at public sale, this picture went for a handful
of silver to an Englishman. And no one interfered ; all the great ones of the city looked on
and saw it done."

His speech had a suppressed fury which I understood and could not help admiring.

" When was this ? " I asked.

" Within the memory of living men. In what other age could it have come to pass ? Years before the king had saved the ' Lesson in Anatomy,' buying it, in private contract, for more than thirty times the paltry sum this brought. But times had changed; pride and self-respect were gone. The nation grovelled in the dust, and clutched its money-bags, while the genius of art wept for shame, with folded wings."

" Why then is this picture here ? It did not go to England. By whom was it saved ? How ? "

" The ship was lost, with all on board," he said mournfully. " Only the picture came to me ; saved as you see it, by a miracle."

" A miracle ! " I answered, with a touch of contempt that I could not restrain. " We have no miracles. Say by accident or by design."

" Or by theft," he added calmly. " That was in your tone."

Our glances met, and I withdrew mine, not without embarrassment. The suspicion had, indeed, occurred to me.

" Have no fear," he continued, with the same sadness. " There was no double-dealing. Wrested from the sea, like this poor land of Holland, the inheritance fell to me honestly. Mine by right, it is here in my possession, and here it shall remain."

"Surely," I objected, "you are not serious. You cannot mean to hide this treasure from the world?"

"The world!" he repeated bitterly. "What is it to me? It has left this picture to become a line in Burger's history. Who knows; who cares; who mourns its loss? The world tramples upon graves."

"That is unjust; if not to all, to one."

"I have no quarrel with you," he returned. "But the money-changers made their price, and it was paid to them. Their treasure is lost beyond recovery. I have sworn it. Then too there is another reason."

"And what is that?" I demanded.

"Look! Can you find nothing there that answers you?"

I turned back to those glowing faces, incomparable in their vivid color, in their strength and beauty. The painter had breathed into them the breath of life; they almost took away my own. Yet his hidden meaning still eluded me.

"No," I sighed; "it is useless, I cannot find the reason."

He had already left me; and as I spoke, he began to put out the lights, one after another, slowly.

"You are so young," he said. "Your eyes have all youth's weakness in them. Patience! they will grow dimmer; you will see."

The light was nearly gone, when, groping with my eyes as with the brain one struggles for the thought it misses, I felt that I was about to catch a glimmering of his secret.

"Wait!" I cried. "One moment more!"

But the last light went out, leaving only the lamp to guide us. It was darkness visible, through which, as before, there rose a group of spectral figures.

"Your time will come," whispered Mynheer Grafman as he unlocked the door. "You said just now, 'We have no miracles;' count it one, hereafter, to have seen the lost Rembrandt."

We stole back into the house with all our former precaution. Everything was as we left it. My host moved back the panel, and put away his lamp and key. It was late; I had no excuse for delaying longer, and bade him good-night. For answer he refilled our empty glasses. I drank the perfumed wine, and once more a grave content benumbed my senses. But I put down the glass and turned to go.

"I can only thank you," I said, "and assure you that I shall always remember these things."

"*Haec olim meminisse*," he murmured. Then, without a smile, without offering his hand, he led the way to the street-door and opened it.

"Good-night!" he said, "and good repose."

Thus, with no hint that we might ever meet again, the door closed upon him. It was a final parting.

I had not overstayed my prescribed limit of time. The quizzical look of the *portier* bore witness to that. But the familiar sights and sounds of the hotel jarred upon me horribly. I could not sink at once to their lower level. I was like one returning home after long absence to find forgotten flaws in everything.

So I went to my room, wide awake, yet half inclined to fancy I was dreaming. Among the few books which had been my only travelling-companions lay a worn copy of Burger's " Dutch Museums." It did not take me long to find his record of the lost picture, — a few lines only, easily overlooked, as I must often have overlooked them. " The color resembles closely that of Titian." Sir Joshua had spoken of it once in those very words. Then followed a statement of the price paid by the Englishman, together with the date of his purchase, — February 7, 1842. " It is astonishing," said the author in conclusion, " that here all knowledge of the picture ends."

I read and reread the paragraph impatiently. It said so little ; but the writer had never seen that of which he wrote. What more could he say ? There was a scrap of paper on the dressing-table. I laughed, remembering how I had left my last instructions upon it. I took it up now to mark the place in the book ; then saw with surprise that this paper was not mine, but that it bore my name in

a strange hand. I opened it and pulled the bell
violently.

"Who brought this?" I asked.

The maid had small English, but was able to
state that she did not know. Whereupon I summoned other servants, until at last I learned that
earlier in the evening an old man had been seen to
knock at my door. He wore livery, and otherwise
the description tallied perfectly with my recollection of the silent familiar who had admitted me to
Mynheer Grafman's house. The messenger was
thus accounted for though not the message.

The paper contained but a line, in faded ink,
lightly written,—

Come to-morrow, three hours after mid-day. I
shall be alone.   ADRIANA.

Nearly all that night I heard the chimes quarter-
ing out the hours. Toward daybreak I slept to
dream of her; and waking, feared to look, lest I
had only dreamed that she had written. But the
letter was still there. At the sight of it my heart
leaped, and then I knew I loved her. What could
those words mean, but that she also knew it and
loved me.

In the clear light of day I reviewed the adventure with all the calmness possible to a man who
has just unlocked his heart's door and found the immortal little bailiff in possession. All my thoughts
led to the same conclusion; and I chafed, impatient

of the hours. The time came at last; and it found me at the house, which now, more than ever, looked like one deserted. The blinds were closed, and there was thick dust upon them. I rang, and got no answer. But the door stood ajar; the afternoon breeze stirred it a little, as if bidding me to go in. "She is alone," I thought, making my way on through the unlighted hall, and finding it very cool and dark to eyes that carried all the sunshine with them. This was the curtained door. As I touched it, low notes of the harp within confirmed me. I waited in the dark one tremulous moment more; then all the light came back, and I saw her there alone.

She sat at the harp, playing softly to herself the air she had played to me. She wore the same colors, even to the white flower at her breast; the surroundings too were all the same. The little table, with the wine, stood exactly where I left it; the present day was carefully shut out; the candles were still burning. There was the pile of music, there the jar of roses; but a few petals had fallen upon the hearth, and the fire had died down into a heap of ashes. While I looked at her I saw these things; for she did not rise, and though her look met mine, she gave me at first no sign of recognition.

I drew nearer, and she welcomed me with her eyes.

"I thought that you would come," she said. "It was much to ask; yet I have more to ask of you."

" I will do all you ask," I answered, " upon one condition." I pointed at the harp. " The song I heard last night, — that is all."

" Listen," she said, and touched the strings.

" Yes," I replied, " it is the same."

" The same air, but with other words. These are in your language."

" And about life ? " I asked.

" Yes, always about life. Listen ! It is called ' In Circe's Garden.' "

There were tears in her voice, — tears too in my eyes. I longed to hear her; yet, at that moment, would have implored her not to sing. The prelude went on softly. There was a cushion on the floor at her side; I flung myself down upon it, half kneeling, half reclining at her feet. But she had forgotten me ; absorbed in the music, with a sweetness that even Circe, the enchantress, might have envied, she sang these words : —

O Love, stay by and sing ;
Thy reddest roses bring,
   Thy richest wine !
I would but fill and quaff,
I would but live and laugh
   And make thee mine!

For Fame 's a field hard-fought,
And gained, a thing of naught
   To have and hold !
Who would the laurel wear
Immortal youth should bear,
   And I am old !

So, Love, stay by and sing,
Thy reddest roses bring,
    Thy richest wine !
I leave the work unwrought,
I leave the field unfought
    For thee and thine !

The song ended.   I forgot its underlying sorrow.
I only knew that with its last notes she turned tenderly to me.   I caught her in my arms and kissed
her.   She broke away with a low cry ; and I drew
back, trembling even in the moment of my triumph,
for my chilled lips had touched a cheek as cold
as marble.   A string in the harp snapped, and one
end came rattling down.   She looked at it and
laughed bitterly.   This sound of mirth, the first
known to me in that strange household, brought an
angry flush into my face.   Once more I was on fire.

"Adriana!" I cried, "do not mock me! Do not
laugh ! I love you."

She sighed, and hid her face in her hands.

"Yes," she said, "I know."

"Why, then, did you bring me here ?   To laugh
at me ? "

"No," she replied.   "Have you forgotten your
promise ? "

"What promise ? "

"Just now, — to do all that I should ask ?"

"I am ready to keep it ! Speak ! What shall
I do ? "

She moved nearer, holding me with a mute appeal which was not to be resisted.   Had she bade

me commit some dreadful crime, I could not have denied her.

"So slight a thing," she said. "Show me what you saw last night."

"What do you mean?"

"The treasure that my father hides from all the world, — even from me."

"The lost picture, — Rembrandt's masterpiece?"

"It is a picture, then. How often I have tried to see it! But the door is always locked, and my father keeps the key, — where, I do not know. But you —"

"Yes," I whispered, turning anxiously to assure myself that we were not overheard. "Yes, I know."

"Do not fear!" she answered. "We are alone. You will let me see it?"

I took a step toward the carved chimney-piece, to find the secret panel, then hesitated a moment longer.

"And afterward?" said I.

She held out her hand to me.

"Afterward," she murmured, "we shall go hand in hand. You will be mine, henceforth; I shall be yours. Though you long to escape, there can be no escaping."

"I shall never long for that," I said, and took her hand. The touch of her fingers sent an icy thrill through all my veins. I seemed to grow sadder and calmer, — years older, in a moment.

There was a new heaviness about my heart; it still remained there after our hands unclasped, — indeed, it has never left me. Yet in spite of it I loved her and shall love her all my days.

I found the panel and pushed it open. I lighted the lamp, while she stood by with questioning eyes and parted lips. Then I took down the key.

"Come!" I said.

I was no longer in her thoughts; they were all for the end and not the means.

"Show it to me!" she whispered eagerly. "Show it to me!"

We went out into the blinding daylight, through the dusty garden to the door of the wine-shop. I opened it, without a word, and went on through the clinging darkness, assured that she would follow. I found the candelabra, and began to light them, still silent, leaving the master to make his own impression upon her. But half the tapers were lighted, when a low moan broke the silence, and turning, I saw her face pale, distorted, with all its beauty faded, in an agony of terror. She spoke no word, but pointed toward the picture, half revealed, and then, with a frightful cry, fled from the place.

Oh horror! The livid figure there upon the canvas was her own. The lovely eyes were closed, the features were sharpened, drawn, distorted, as I had just now seen them. But the face was hers, — dead, dead; only waiting for the grave. She had recognized it; she had learned the secret, and now I saw it too.

I dropped the lamp and rushed back into the sunshine. There was no sign of her; but the long window, which we had carefully closed behind us, stood open, as she must have left it in her flight. I hurried after her, up the broken steps, over the crumbling terrace, into the room. She was not there; but on the floor I found the white camellia, lying where it had fallen from her breast. I caught it up; its petals were already stained and withered. I saw an ugly worm wriggling in their folds; and I dropped the poor, decaying flower with a shiver of disgust.

I looked around me. A shadow had fallen upon the room. The glare of day had blighted it, even as the white camellia had been blighted. The candles writhed in their sockets, sputtering and flaring and going out, one by one. The drops of the rusted sconces hung lustreless; the pictures showed centuries of blackness on them; their frames were tarnished; the splendid hangings too were musty and worm-eaten. The very floor felt rotten under my feet. Something rustled along the wainscot; it was only a hungry rat slinking back to his hole.

"Adriana!" I called. "Adriana!" and the walls mocked me with her nickname, — "Yanna! Yanna!"

I rushed out into the hall, dislodging, as I went, the heavy curtain, which fell in shreds about my heels. I climbed the creaking stairs, still calling her by name, entreating her to answer. Above were locked doors that I could not open. One at last gave way, crashing down into a chamber empty but for an old bedstead with a tattered canopy. The broken window-panes were choked with cobwebs. Dust rose in clouds. Then, all at once, the loneliness appalled me. I dashed down the staircase to the street-door, on the threshold shouting back once more into the silence; and once more my voice returned to me that dismal echo, — "Yanna! Yanna!"

I took to the streets like a thief in desperation, spurred on by a new fear, bent upon a new purpose. I had no time to lose, for my objective point was the Mauritshuis, which in a few minutes would be closed for the day. I found the last visitors departing; the doorkeeper smiled as he pulled out his watch, but I passed him by breathlessly, and went up, at breakneck speed, two stairs at a time, to the Rembrandt room. I stood before the "Lesson in Anatomy;" and shutting out the surgeons with my hand, looked only at their recumbent subject. There could be no longer any doubt. The face was set and rigid, — lengthened, sunken, blank, and expressionless, like all dead faces. But I knew it now for Mynheer Grafman's.

Excited and alarmed, I dared not look behind me, lest I should find him at my shoulder, where I had seen him first. I shut my eyes and groped my way to the door ; then felt for the stair-rail, as a blind man would have done. Only when I heard the custodian's chatter did I recover sight; only in the open air could I breathe freely.

How to account for all this noise and shouting in the great square? The sober Hollanders had lost their self-control for once. A herd of them flew by me like wild deer, across the gravel in the direction of the Spui. I gave chase at once, determined to be in at the death, if that were possible. But my haste got the better of me, and before I could check myself, I had plumped into the waistcoat of a big Dutchman, who bore down upon me adversely with ponderous swiftness. He stopped to take breath, swinging me round like a cat. It was only the giant *portier* of the Marshal Turenne.

" What is the matter ? " I gasped.

He was in no condition to talk.

" Fire ! " was all he said. " Fire ! This way, — come ! " and we plunged on together.

In a few seconds I longed for wings. We turned from the Spui into the narrow street thrice familiar to me. I knew where we were going. My guilty cry passed unnoticed in the increasing uproar, but it might have given evidence against myself. I had opened doors and windows upon fifty candle-flames. I had dropped a lighted lamp into a tinder-box. I knew where we were going. The angry cloud of smoke above us interpreted my fear.

Our way was already blocked. It soon became impassable. Then my companion turned off into a maze of by-streets and slimy, green canals, I following blindly. We made a long détour, crossing bridge after bridge, and coming out into the crowd again ; but the friendly giant ploughed a furrow in it with his shoulders, dragging me behind him. And he did not stop until, with inarticulate murmurs of satisfaction, he had set me up like a tenpin directly in front of the burning house, but on the opposite wall of the canal. One — two — three — four — five. I counted again and again. I had guessed it. The house was the fifth from the corner.

I saw files of men handing water in buckets, others working madly at primitive hand-engines ; but the case was obviously desperate. Before I had recovered my breath, the roof fell in, and a shaft of flame shot up into the sky.

Near us, in the crowd, a workman stood talking and gesticulating to his neighbor, and as the best of us will do under excitement, repeating over and over the same words.

" What does he say ? " I asked the *portier.*

The man listened a moment, then translated the speech.

" He says it is a good thing. The house was haunted."

" What ?   Listen again.   Are you sure ? "

" Yes," repeated the *portier,* after another pause.

" The house was haunted.   No one has lived in it
since thirty years."

" Impossible ! " I cried.

The man misunderstood me of course.

" Impossible, perhaps, in your country.   Here
we have ghosts," he said with the serenity of
conviction.

I did not dispute the point, and we stood still
for some time huddled together in an ill-assorted
group of all ages, sizes, and conditions.   The fire
roared and crackled ; the sashes of the drawing-
room were like the bars of a grate ; all within was
a live coal.   I stared at it vacantly, with the refrain
of that unearthly music moaning in my ears.

At last I turned again to the interpreter.

" Ask the fellow," I said, " if he has ever heard
of one Heer Grafman, living here in the quarter."

" What for a name is that ? " the *portier* asked.

" Grafman, — Mynheer Grafman."

" Excuse me ; one must have made a mistake,
— that cannot be the name."

" Why not, pray ? "

" There was no name like that in our language.
In Dutch that means — "

" What ? " I urged impatiently.

" It means ' one come out of the grave.' "

" You are right," said I ; " there has been some
mistake.   You need not ask.   That cannot be the
name."

There is no more to tell. A few days later I left The Hague ; I have not revisited Holland, and all this happened years ago. It is a ghost of my lost youth, but one that never can be laid. Often in the summer night, I hear that saddest and sweetest of all songs in a troubled dream from which my own despairing cry arouses me ; and I wake in tears, to find myself calling, " Yanna ! Adriana ! " I can listen to no other music ; for me, on earth, there is no love of woman. The old delight I had in living has been taken from me ; but, at least, I live on calmly and no longer dread the end. All fear of Death is gone, — I know no touch of it. I only know that I looked into those quiet eyes, and that I ceased to find them terrible.

OUT OF NEW ENGLAND GRANITE.

She, though in full-blown flower of glorious beauty,
Grows cold, even in the summer of her age.
                            LEE and DRYDEN: *Œdipus.*

I.

HE will never forget his first sight of her.
Half-unconsciously she had drawn apart
from one of the merry groups on the lawn, to stand
for the moment alone, looking up at the stars, awed
a little by the beauty of the perfect July evening.
The moonlight streamed down upon her golden
hair; upon her face, which, if not wholly faultless,
had faultless lines in it and was gentleness itself;
while the pale blue-and-white Eastern fabric that
she wore gave her slender figure an unearthly look,
making it seem like an effect of the moonshine,
ready to melt away if one drew nearer. But
other figures came and went between her and the
wide expanse of glimmering sea. Two of them
joined her, — two men ; and she did not vanish,
but smiled and spoke with them. Though he could
not hear the words, he caught the sweet tones of
her voice, saw the smile clearly, and wished it were

for him.   He had met more beautiful women, perhaps, — none more interesting at the first glance,
he was sure.   At the thought he sighed without
knowing it.   One of the men had handed her a
rose.

His friend Mordaunt must always smoke his two
cigars after dinner, though the sky fell ; and so
they had come late to Mrs. Shirley Allerton's midsummer " Small-and-early."   His hostess had led
him out of her reception-room to this dark corner
of the veranda, that he might discover at once how
admirably Nature chimed in with all her schemes
of artificial entertainment.   On the whole sweep of
Massachusetts Bay there is no choicer bit of coast-
line than North Head, and she wanted him to tell
her so.   A few yards out, above a sunken rock, a
great white breaker perpetually rose and fell, —
her breaker, she called it.   And, indeed, it seemed
to be always the same wave, always tumbling over
and over there at her command.   That was her
moon too while it lasted ; she could not have that
always.   Even the wife of Allerton, the eminent
historian, all-powerful in her social world, lost her
control of things, and confessed herself baffled
and valueless, somewhere just on this side of the
spheres.

From a distant room, where there was dancing,
faint notes of harp and violin came out to them,
and mingled with the deeper music of the shore.
Her guest undertook to admire all the sights and

sounds she indicated, and he did so, for the moment, heartily. Then, suddenly, while she talked on, his look and thought were arrested on the wing.

" Lovely ! " he murmured in an undertone which expressed more and less than that he had before employed.

His hostess saw what he meant, and smiled. " Yes, is n't she ? That is Sylvia Belknap. Come ! I want you to know her." And moving out toward the little group she continued, in the same breath : " Miss Belknap, my old friend, Mr. Luxmore, who has just come home to us again."

The men drew back, one of them proving to be Allerton himself ; the second, only Mordaunt, Luxmore's bosom friend. Another group formed, and in its turn, broke up ; so that presently the two just introduced were left alone. Luxmore, looking at his companion, felt vague relief at that and at something else. It was Allerton who had given her the rose.

At that time Luxmore's work had its small circle of friendly critics who discerned signs of promise in it ; but he was an unknown painter to the great mass of humankind. Even those who liked his pictures so well as to buy them, at low prices, never ventured to predict for him what is called " a future ; " and in their saner moments they could only feel that their money, represented by his few feet of decorative canvas, was safely put out of the way. To be sure he knew how to draw

the human figure, and his bits were strong in
color; he had passed several years in Paris and
had improved his advantages. That he had talent
was obvious from their recognition of him; but he
also had an income enabling him to live,—frugally,
it is true, but still to live. He was a slow worker,
with a tendency to doubt himself that often brought
down upon him the reproach of indolence. His
annual product was ridiculously small. He had
come back this time to stay, as every decent American of his age should do, of course. But here, at
thirty-five, with his temperament, important work
could hardly be expected of him. A good-humored,
handsome fellow, always well-met in society, he
would be to the end of the chapter. Yet in his
art, it was more than likely that his best word had
been already spoken.

His mother had died when he was very young;
he could but just remember her. He was the only
child, left in the care of a father who was easy-
going and indulgent. The boy had grown up like
a weed, making no mark in college other than the
score of his debts, which had led to more or less
trouble at home. But after the reproof the money
was always forthcoming; and his father sorrowfully
admitted to himself that, on the whole, his son's
youth was steadier than his own had been. All
boys were wild, he supposed; but time would cure
that. His boy's heart was in the right place.
He must have his fling. As for the money,

there would be enough in the end, if things went well.

But the end came suddenly, and things went ill. The father died without a moment's warning, the estate proved to be heavily involved, and Luxmore was left high and dry with a small income, helped out only by the trifling sum inherited from his mother. This change sobered him at once. His fling was over. He determined now to make the most of a serious existence; whatever enjoyment was to be found in it should be his. And having artistic tastes and qualities, he chose the painter's profession, for the love of it, not for its precarious reward. If he succeeded, why, well and good; if not, he would burn his brushes, take up the pen, and turning critic, instruct and irritate the successful. Even failure thus might bring in its compensations. But these must be his last resort; he was not disposed to fall back upon them just yet.

Nor did he ever need in this manner to call his reserve forces into play. The difficult task of setting the world on fire had yet to be accomplished. But if his work never went very far, it was always thorough; and the limited following to which he appealed respected him through all the hours of self-distrust that now succeeded. He had served a long apprenticeship of preparation for a higher flight. When his friends urged the attempt upon him, he only shook his head; till gradually they came to fear that he would never make it. The

torch had been passed on to him, undoubtedly, with
the spark still glowing. Why did he not draw one
deep breath and kindle that shining point into a
flame ?

It is always easy to defend with a wise proverb
any defect or idiosyncrasy of our own. And Luxmore might well have answered these spiritual
inciters that, in hastening slowly, he was but obey-
ing an important precept of the sages, another of
whose laws he endeavored with zealous devotion to
fulfil. He studied himself assiduously, as do all
good artists, whatever be the medium in which
they work. And in consequence, far from shielding himself with a delusive epigram, he went, as
has already been intimated, straight to the opposite
extreme, and was inclined to undervalue himself.
Certain elements were entirely wanting in him, as
he had reason to fear. How had he done so much
without them ? The wonder was that he could do
anything at all ?

Love, for instance, still remained an unknown
quantity in his personal experience. Was he, then,
never to feel the racking torment, the unutterable
sorrow, the inexpressible joy that poets have rung
their changes on these thousand years ? One by
one his friends had dropped away, confiding to him,
as they went, their woes and their delights, to which
he had listened with an amiable, unsympathetic
smile. Wait till you are caught, they had retorted ;
and he had smiled again, incredulously, envying

them, wondering at them. His own boyish fancies of the past had been quite too unimportant to confide at all; even to recall them demanded a positive effort of the mind, turning back through countless blank leaves of intervening years during which the little shameless bowman had never revealed himself to Luxmore; never drawn a single arrow from the quiver upon his account; never stooped to brush him by with so much as the tip of a wing.

What did it mean? Had the heart for love been left out of him, as the eye for color is from one man, the ear for music from another? If so, to the winds with all ambitious strivings; undoubtedly, thought he, love has played its part in all lives that were worthy to be written. Not to love was not to soar; to be a creature of earth, not the eagle, but the strutting monarch of the dunghill, — inferior to him, even, for the barnyard fowl has wings that he might use, if he were so minded. To want wings altogether was to be cruelly handicapped. To find the highest of all earthly conditions incomprehensible seemed equivalent to an admission of mediocrity. Commonplace was the only term applicable to such a nature. And as the nature, so the work must be.

This conclusion, lamentable as it sounded, should have been his encouragement; since the true grovelling spirit is content to grovel and does not concern itself with whys and wherefores. It might also have led him (though, happily or unhappily, it

did nothing of the kind) to ask himself precisely
how far this apparent invulnerability was to be
trusted in a close encounter. The vigorous man
who has never known a day's illness suffers most
when the fever strikes him down ; and love is the
most insidious and malignant of all fevers. Its
germs are flying everywhere. From eighteen to
eighty, none of us is really safe one hour. Nay,
more ; it may safely be asserted that none ever
escapes a serious attack of it. And all in vain the
scoffer would confute this with shining instances
of celibacy like Lord Macaulay and Leonardo da
Vinci. These were strong, wise men, who burned
their documents, who locked their feelings up and
flung away the key. But on that final day when
all hearts shall be laid bare, love's scars surely will
be found even upon these. The hermit shows you
his cell triumphantly, and assures you it is an open
book, thus telling the truth with intent to deceive ;
for his book proves to be written in a strange
character that he alone can read. Though the
skull and hour-glass are his only obvious furniture,
they form, in fact, a very small portion of the
baggage buried with him in the cloister.

Luxmore, as it happened, was neither sage nor
hero, and in a few moments Miss Belknap skilfully
contrived to make him do the thing of all others
he usually desired to avoid, — namely, to talk about
himself. But to-night he was off his guard ; and
his companion, provokingly sympathetic, put intel-

ligent questions that showed her knowledge of the
art he pursued to be something more than a theo-
retic one. Of his individual work she knew nothing whatever. This disappointed him a little, but
it did not surprise him. A Luxmore, to be sure,
hung in the very house behind them. But one
might pass it by a dozen times unnoticed, or notice
it only to forget it, he supposed. In answer to his
question she admitted that she could draw and
paint in a small way for her own amusement. And
then she turned the talk straight back to him, and
made him tell her of his life abroad, of the strange
people he had met there, the friends he had found,
— the better to listen leading him away from the
music and the dancers, along the cliff, to a turn in
the path where a bench had been placed fronting
the sea and just out of sight of the house. Here,
with Mrs. Allerton's breaker tossing high its foam
before him, Luxmore revived recollections that,
beginning joyously, ended by having a mournful
note in them, as such recitals are apt to do. And
both the joy and the sadness were echoed by the
girl at his side, whose interest in all he said was
quite unfeigned, and who had already become a
part of his life. He had known her half an hour,
yet he seemed to have known her always; the
acquaintance had but just begun, and they were
old friends.

They had been speaking of the "painters' painters," as Luxmore called them, — the men whom

their fellows agree in admiring, whose sketches are
treasured in dim studio corners, but whose completed work fails to touch the public heart, or
gains tardy appreciation only when the hand and
brain that toiled for it are beyond the need of
toiling.   A common fate enough.   All the arts,
in all the ages, have developed such builders for
posterity, and their great triumphal arch is still
unfinished.

"Yes," said Luxmore, " I believe that we should
all fare better to live upon the fruits of our an-
cestors, sealing up our own rare products for a
later generation.   Some men, it is true, learn how
to hit the present; but others never can, — then
death sweeps them away into the past, and behold,
they are immortal!   There was a poor friend of
mine who died last year, obscure, unrecognized.
To-day, at the sales, the amateurs wrangle for two
strokes of his brush.   I wonder if he knows?"

"Was he an American?" Miss Belknap asked.

"Yes, though not a good one.   Something, I
don't know what, led him to forsake his native
land for a French village in the forest of Saint
Germain.   Once there he never left it.   Those who
cared for him had to seek him out.   But they were
always sure of a welcome and something more.
There was much in the man worth studying besides patience and frugality.   Yet he called us his
master-pupils, and declared that, in our game of
give and take, the advantage was all his."

Miss Belknap opened her fan and gently smoothed its ruffled feathers.

"What was the name of your recluse?" she inquired.

"It will say nothing to you, for no one here remembers him. And yet he used to tell me that he had left his masterpiece in America; his first sketch for it is mine now. I would give the world to see the picture. But how shall I? A needle in a haystack! One might look from here to San Francisco and never find it. Why do you laugh?"

"Because you have quite forgotten my question. No matter, I will answer it. The painter's name was Selden."

Luxmore started.

"How did you know?"

"From your description of course. And the picture you would give the world to see is a flying wood-nymph. Well, give me the world, and I will show it to you."

"No," said Luxmore, laughing, "you will show it to me for nothing, if you are charitable."

Miss Belknap rose and caught up the silken coil of her train.

"Shall we go now?" she asked.

"By all means, — but where?"

"Do you see those lights upon the shore? No, the others, farther off. That is my house; the picture is there. Come!"

Springing lightly down the path as she spoke, she looked back for him to follow.

"Wait a moment. Let me bring your wrap," said he.

"Come!" she repeated, stamping her foot impatiently. "Or I shall change my mind, and you will never see the picture. It is but a step, — in ten minutes we can be there and back again. Take care; you will break your neck."

The way was so narrow that they could not walk abreast. So he followed her obediently, by trim lawns and gardens that swept back to lamp-lit houses on one side, while on the other the summer surf advanced and retreated lazily, then bounded back almost to her feet. Its phosphorescent gleams seemed to play about her; she gained upon him, disappearing and shining out again fitfully, like a will-o'-the-wisp of the sea. He begged her to stop, and found her waiting at a turnstile, through which they passed, over turf that felt like velvet to a large, old-fashioned house, well lighted, with doors and windows wide open. In one of the ground-floor rooms sat a placid, middle-aged woman, knitting under a lamp. As they went by she looked up.

"Sylvia!" she called.

"Yes," replied the girl, but without stopping led the way into a hall crowded with curious objects, like some cabinet in a fine museum. Luxmore had only a confused impression of these

things, as he was hurried along into a dark corridor behind, where Miss Belknap kept him waiting while she found a candle and lighted it, going
on immediately to a closed door, which she unlocked and opened to admit him, like a willing
dog at her heels.

He stopped a moment on the threshold, for there
was no other light than the uncertain one she carried. The room was bare, and plainly furnished,
with a forsaken look and chilly air, as though it
were rarely used. On the wall he caught a glimpse
of the picture they had come to see. Then Miss
Belknap, who had moved toward it, gave a startled
exclamation, scarcely audible, which she at once
suppressed, and the candle went out, — with her
help he was sure. He heard her rustling forward
in the dark. The shutters were closed, but one of
their upper leaves had unfolded, letting a bar of
moonlight slant down close by the picture upon the
wall and upon her as she came out into it, putting
up her hand toward the frame with a quick movement that he could not follow. She was there
and gone again in a flash, coming back to him
and laughing.

" How stupid! " she said, as if to show him that
the light had gone out by accident. " Now I must
find the bell, if I can, and ring for matches."

" No! Take mine! " said Luxmore, offering his
match-box with one hand, and groping for her with
the other. He touched her face, her hair; but she

slipped away, and kneeling down, let him go by
her, as though it were a game of blind-man's-buff.

" Where are you ?" he cried, in the moonlight
now, but more in the dark than ever.

" Here !" she answered in a laughing whisper,
close behind him. Then she took his hand and
placed the candle in it. And between them, with
some difficulty, the flame flashed up again. What
was there in his look, he wondered, that made her
change color and turn away from it. He had not
been thinking of himself. But now, as he did so,
he felt for the first time that he was in danger.

Selden was quite right. He had never done
anything so good as this poor little nymph, flying
breathless from some unseen pursuer. Even in
the insufficient light Luxmore was convinced of
that. The quality of the flesh, the modelling, the
color, the composition, were all remarkable.

" Poor Selden !" he muttered, after a long look
in silence. This was like seeing a ghost, and when
Miss Belknap, who had stood aside, watching him,
suggested that lamps should be brought, he would
not hear of it. He was not sure of himself ; there
were tears in his eyes.

" After all, it is always there," she said. " You
will see it by day, I hope."

" Yes ; I shall be glad to come."

His tone struck her. She held the light above
her head in a becoming attitude, looking at him
curiously.

"A little for the picture, — a little too for me. We have had such a pleasant talk. There are many things I want to ask you. I am sure we shall be friends."

"We are already," said he, taking the hand she offered, with a smile. Then, as she turned to go, he sprang forward quickly and opened the door. In doing this he felt that his foot was entangled in some light substance that clung persistently.

"What have I brought with me?" he asked, holding up a knot of crape with flying ends that had wound themselves about his ankle. "A badge of mourning?"

"It is nothing," she said indifferently. "Let it lie there, — anywhere. Will you lock the door and give me the key? Make haste; we are playing truant, — we belong to-night to Mrs. Shirley Allerton."

As they walked back Luxmore was silent, dropping behind again. At the end of the path she turned upon him with a playful reproach.

"Not one word?" she said. "You are gloomy as the grave."

"It is your own fault," he answered; "you set the current of my thoughts." And after a pause, when they came within hearing of the music, within sight of the dancers, he added, "So you knew Selden?"

She smiled, speaking lightly, but in a tone that betrayed some slight embarrassment. "Oh, yes.

I thought I told you. I had a great regard for
him. Here comes the best waltzer in the world.
Do you think he means to dance with me ? Yes;
you are released. But you won't forget the way
to my door, will you ? "

She went off with the other man, and Luxmore,
returning to the bench where they had talked
together, sat there for a while alone.

" A great regard!" he thought. " That's the
sort of thing a woman says of the poor dog who
has had his day with her. I wonder if Selden lost
his head and returned her regard with interest.
That would explain him. She had tied the bit of
crape about his picture, and was ashamed to let me
see it. Why? Now that he is safe she cares for
him too much perhaps. And I am winding myself
up with thoughts as melancholy as the crape itself.
She was right. I am gloomy as the grave. If I
were superstitious I should call it a bad omen to
have Selden's mantle fall on me. But my head is
sound as a nut, and I am safe, — entirely safe. The
devil take her ! What do I care about the girl ?"

Then he walked up to the ball-room window
and saw her for the first time in a good light.
She was older than he had thought, — twenty-five
or twenty-six, he dared say. Yes, she might well
have had that little affair with Selden. How grace-
fully she danced ! The younger girls were conscious and awkward in comparison with her, —
mere jointed dolls. Others beside himself were

following with their looks the golden hair, the clear, blue, laughing eyes. When she stopped, a small court formed about her, cutting her off from view. Then Luxmore, gloomier than ever, went into the house, and keeping out of her way forced himself to say cheerful nothings wittily to the first good soul he met. So he passed on from one old friend to another, till the clouds lifting left him in a better frame of mind. If not precisely a full-grown lion, he was looked upon as one of the whelps; and he could not be wholly insensible to that deference which poor humanity always pays to the lords of the menagerie. Later he found himself once more comparing notes with his hostess.

" Well, did you like her ?" she inquired.

" Whom do you mean ? "

" Sylvia, — Miss Belknap, of course."

" Perfection, — but for one fault. She does not know my work."

" Poor sensitive plant! You have the vice of genius. You are exactly like my husband."

" Agreed, with thanks; but that is neither here nor there."

" Oh, but it is. Her fault may be overcome."

" I am not so sure of that," said he. " Tell me — " he had a question about Miss Belknap on his lips and behind it a dozen others. But he suppressed them all, and asked something altogether different. On the whole he preferred to get his information elsewhere.

II.

THE opportunity came an hour afterward when
he and Mordaunt exchanged their impressions
of the evening, in loose attire, over a final cigar.
John Mordaunt rolled through the world in wealth,
the type of jollity. He was short and round and
ruddy; bald as a globe; with a nimble wit; and
an inner man so nicely adjusted to his outer one
that he was happy in himself, and in all things
appertaining to him. His wife and children were
the best that ever lived; his house in town was
the most comfortable that could be contrived,
if not the grandest; his country-house and this
again at North Head fell little behind it in his
own estimation, and were in fact admirably well-
ordered. He prided himself upon his social judg-
ments, incisively pronounced and dangerously
true, — so that those who did not like him had a
wholesome fear of him; and his blunt sincerity made
him troops of friends. He was fond of quoting Sir
Peter's conclusions about sentiment, a disposition
of the mind which he attributed to dyspepsia; but
he stated this so often as to betray a conscious
weakness of his own in that respect, especially in
view of the fact that his courtship had been a sentimental one, and that he had grown domestic to
the last degree. He had long been intimate with
Roger Luxmore, whom he admired for the imagi-

native qualities which were lacking in himself. He had none of the creative faculty, but was a born critic, whose powers ran to waste. Unfortunately he could live without cultivating them, without application to hard labor of any kind. It was only to quiet his conscience that he took his ease in his office and dabbled in the law.

Luxmore knew that his friend must have definite views about so important a figure as Miss Belknap already appeared to him to be. But while he was preparing his first ingenious question, Mordaunt, without warning, plunged straight into the heart of the subject.

"What did you think of Lady Sylvia?" he asked. "I saw her making off with you."

"Not wholly unattractive," said Luxmore, cautiously; "and with a good eye for color, — she wore just the right one."

"I am glad it's no worse. She did not, then, intoxicate you?"

"You forget that I'm an old bird," said Luxmore, smiling; "the wine I drink must be made of grapes. But tell me something about her. Seriously, she did interest me a little."

"Then mark my words. Beware of her. She is hard as flint, and will never be otherwise; for she inherited hardness as she did her money. Her father and grandfather before her were mere ossifications."

Of these words Luxmore marked only one. He

had often sworn to himself that, come what might, he would never ask a rich woman to be his wife, and now his heart sank. "What!" he thought. "Do I love her, then, already?"

"So she has money," was all he said aloud.

"Coffers, Roger, coffers. And she is charitable too in her way; she subscribes well. But no fortune-hunter will ever spend one penny of it; no good fellow lives that will ever share it with her. Make a note of that; you will see."

"I see that you take a great deal for granted," returned Luxmore, laughing.

"Laugh if you like, you don't know her as I do. You have lived in France, where the women, with all their faults, are women still. God bless them, every one, I say; but not a type like this, which is getting to be far too common here at home. There's no sentimental nonsense about me, you may be sure, but I want a woman to be tender and gentle, and to show a proper weakness, — in short, to be flesh and blood, and not a cold abstraction. The girls nowadays seem to think that their only duty is to improve their minds. They refine themselves to death; they won't look at a man, they want a demi-god. He never comes; and they live single and passionless, die, and bury their talent in the grave. What good have they done the world with all their delightful intellectuality? They were born to hand it down. It's their only excuse for being."

" Your happy household is your best argument," said Luxmore; " but think of the risk they run in saying ' yes.' Look around you at the unhappy marriages."

" Nonsense. The man runs his risk, does n't he? Why not the woman? Because she is too self-centred; she will not let herself go a single instant. What we call love implies some sacrifice; she would not make it if she could. Look at the case in point. Here is Sylvia Belknap, young, lovely, rich beyond reckoning. She has no near relatives; she lives alone with her servants and her companion, Miss Winchester. It is the most selfish and limited of lives. She writes her checks, studies her art and her philosophy, cuts the leaves of her review, dines, dances, and her day is done. Unluckily her coldness, that should repel, attracts. More than one better man than she deserves to get, has dangled after her and come to grief. She cannot understand it, she has improved all antiquated ideas away. I have no patience with such a temperament. Her smile makes me think of a vein of quartz in its granite setting. She is like that reef out there, — the waves rush at it, and the biggest can only dash itself to pieces. What are you laughing at now?"

" Only to think that the gods made Mordaunt poetical."

" Fudge ! " said Mordaunt, flinging away his cigar, and bustling about to lock the windows.

" It takes a good strong simile to touch you ; and
you are a little on my conscience. I want to see
you married, — though not to Lady Sylvia, as my
wife persists in calling her. Ugh ! East wind,
again ! After all that girl is the natural product
of our cursed climate. Had she been born with
feelings, ten to one they would have been chilled
out of her. Past two o'clock ! ' And so to bed,'
as Pepys says."

Mordaunt's random shot about similes was really
apt enough. It would have taken one far stronger
than any he had invented to make a deep impression upon Luxmore in this instance. Well begun
is more than half done in matters of the heart.
The affections, once engaged, benumb the reason.
No two men can agree precisely concerning the
color of an object. They do not see it with the
same eyes. And their views are even more at
variance in the discussion of a character. There is
no rule of proportion accurately to determine that.
The lines which to one are clear and well defined
are blurred and iridescent to the other. Sharp attack provokes skilful defence ; and argument, usually
profitless, here becomes absolutely futile. To warn
a man against a woman on whom his eyes have once
looked longingly is to raise up for her a champion.

So the friendly caution went in at one ear and
out at the other, dismissed by Luxmore as an
absurd bit of social prejudice the moment Miss
Belknap's influence exerted itself again. Of course

she had her suitors; how could she help that? Of
course she would marry when the right man came
along; how could any one suppose the contrary?
To choose wisely was her affair; not to choose at
all would be her misfortune, rather than the world's.
She lived in a land of liberty. No law, written or
unwritten, could compel her to marry for the sake
of pleasing the bystanders. The doctrine of hered-
ity was well enough, if well worked out; but who
could describe its limits, verify its laws? What
would it matter that her father and grandfather
had been cut in adamant, if some forgotten ancestor, blessed with a warm heart, had transmitted
his gentleness to her?

These reflections followed hard upon the visit
Luxmore paid her, ostensibly for the purpose of
seeing Selden's nymph by day. The abandoned
room had been opened to the air and sunlight; but
there had been no other attempt to make it habita-
ble. On a table were scattered brushes and tubes
of color; in one corner stood an empty easel. Her
work was not worth showing, she said; she had
given it all up now; some day, perhaps, she might
try again, more seriously. If there were only some
one to help her out. She felt the need of a good
master, — the incentive that men acquired in a
Parisian atelier. She was glad to hear that he had
taken a studio in town. His influence would be of
the best, she knew. Directly and indirectly a man
of high aims always did so much. By the force of

his example he would teach others to desire something more than money-getting, to strive for an ideal.

Thus flattered and humored Luxmore yielded to
the spell of her potent personality, and carried
away with him a glowing sense of its charm. The
glow still remained when he dined at her house a
few days afterward. It was one of those quiet little dinners of general conversation with congenial
people that survive in memory the pomp of a formal
banquet. Luxmore sat between Miss Belknap and
Mrs. Shirley Allerton. He was in high spirits and
talked freely and well; so well that Allerton moved
round to him after dinner, and told him tales of
his youth, informing his wife, on the way home,
that Luxmore was a fine fellow whom she must
corral often when they went to town.

"It is some one else who will corral him, as you
call it, Shirley."

"To whom do you refer?"

"Can't you see? Sylvia, of course."

"Oh!" replied her husband, in blank amazement.
"You are very far-sighted, my dear."

"Not at all. How can you talk so? I have
decided that it would be a most excellent thing.
In fact, I have set my heart upon it."

"Then it will be, my dear, without the slightest
question."

But many moons waxed and waned, and still
it was not. More than that, Luxmore, sitting
up one autumn night over his fire, took strange

counsel with himself, and decided that it could never be. He had been thinking far too much, lately, of Miss Belknap, — or of her fortune, which was it? Overwhelmed by a new impalpable force beyond his comprehension he strove against it, now refusing to admit it at all, now ascribing it to an unworthy motive, and struggling merely to conquer that, as he believed. What! Marry to forfeit his independence? Clinging to a woman's skirts, to decline upon inglorious ease? Impossible! No man could do that and respect himself; better an empty purse than a full one in the wrong hand. Men were born to lead, not to follow. And yet, if he were doing himself grave injustice; if this nameless longing were of a kind to hold through all changes of material, outward circumstance, — if she were penniless, for instance, would he not still long for her? Ah, how could he be sure of that? She had always worn the golden cestus. Who could say that it contributed nothing to her mysterious, indefinable charm? The merest shadow of a doubt deprived him of the right to speak. And doubt, he argued, was inseparable from these conditions. Long he considered them; so long, that the fire died away unheeded, and through his high window came the first glimmer of the dawn. He roused himself, shivering, to shut it out, and sleep. The silent debate was over; its question was answered in the negative.

Resolutely, then, he set his face against temptation. He could not avoid Miss Belknap altogether, of course; but he no longer made an effort to meet her. When they were thrown together his talk was of the lightest and marked by an odd nervousness of manner. He was continually contriving that they should not be left alone. Thus it happened that, for one reason or another, she was always in his thoughts, and the chosen pursuit which should have absorbed them found but a secondary place. His winter was restless and unprofitable. He attempted no important work, but under a growing discouragement, yielded to the fancied claims of society, kept its late hours, and paid the penalty, — by day, tilting at his own poor windmills with a tired hand. Nevertheless the studies he turned out sold readily. Chance and his tact in dealing with it had made him the favorite of the hour; for the hour, it was the thing to encourage him.

With charming inconsistency his friend Mrs. Shirley Allerton alternately reproached him for wasting his time, and by her own tempting invitations made sad inroads upon it. When he laughingly called her attention to this fact, she had her answer ready. No man, in her judgment, should be permitted to immure himself. Until he was married and settled, which change for the better, according to her emphatic parenthesis, should always occur on the hither side of forty,

he must see people; not all people, of course,
not the dull and conventional, but the wise and
clever, — in short, the right ones. Then, to point
her moral, she asked him to dinner, and made
him take Miss Belknap in. But some one had
failed her at the last moment. The place on
his left hand was vacant. For that reason, no
doubt, Sylvia took pains to be doubly captivating.
She began with a flattering complaint. In long
weeks she had seen nothing of him; she could
hardly remember when they had talked together
as they were talking now. This argued, evidently,
that he was hard at work. Indeed she had been
shown the results, and she could well understand
that art should be his first thought; but it need
not be his only one; he must think sometimes '
of — his friends.

He had thought of them too often, as he was on
the point of saying. But he checked himself and
turned the conversation off into impersonalities.
She followed where he led her, listening with an
attentive smile, making her own points cleverly
but deferentially. How well their tastes agreed!
How plainly she expressed her hope in his success
without the aid of one insipid compliment; her
pleasure in his companionship without an atom's
loss of maidenly reserve! What warmth of sympathy was hers, what delicacy of feeling! Refinement was in all her looks and gestures; her voice
had nothing of the world's harshness, — every note

of it was an appeal. The hours of that night fled like minutes; but they left behind them an eternity of recollection.

"A fine stroke of yours, that vacant place!" said Mr. Allerton to his wife, when their guests were gone.

"Now, Shirley, please, for once, do me justice."

"How am I unjust? In giving you credit for benevolent diplomacy?"

"Match-making isn't that. It's unwarrantable interference, more likely to do harm than good. I detest it thoroughly, as you ought to know. You can't push people into marriage and expect them to be happy. Miss Burleigh really gave out at the last moment. I couldn't have filled her place if I had tried."

"My dear, I apologize. But with nobody on his left, and somebody on his right — "

"Well, why shouldn't he take her in?"

"He couldn't help himself; and any event that may occur will be purely fortuitous. There is a special providence that waits on lovers."

"Lovers!" repeated his wife, laughing and then sighing. "Nothing will occur; I am out of patience. But I shall never interfere," she concluded with determination.

For a long time Mrs. Allerton's rash prediction was borne out by the fact, and nothing did occur in this important matter, which, as she had before confessed, was very near her heart. All the fol-

lowing summer and well into the autumn, Luxmore still strove to do what he conceived to be his
duty; namely, to forget the woman whose accident
of wealth weighed upon him, warping his better
judgment, making his love an oppressive and tormenting burden. Then came the inevitable moment when he ceased to struggle, and like a tired
swimmer, let the current have its way. It swept
him on fiercely. And now, in the world, he was
always at her side, completing the tedious round
of so-called pleasures for her sake, lightly. Out
of her sight, he carried her image with him; but
he was no longer unhappy, for he no longer argued
with himself. If the old problem crept into his
mind, he dismissed it with a word. "Time must
settle it," he now decided. And when a man says
that in such a case, he uses time in a special sense,
and its true meaning is opportunity.

For her part, Sylvia met his advances kindly.
More than that, her face brightened when he approached; when he rose to go, she entreated him
to stay. The world began to interpret these signs
in its own reckless fashion, and to leave them more
and more to themselves. One night they had been
alone for hours in a crowded drawing-room; as the
guests took leave they fell into line together; then
he led her down, ordered her carriage, and went
back for her to the cloak-room door. As she came
out, drawing her furs about her, some roses fell
from her dress. Luxmore caught them.

"What is it?" she asked. "My fan, my hand-kerchief? No; here they are."

"Only these," said Luxmore; she held out her hand to take the flowers, but he shook his head. "Let me keep them."

"Bring me them to-morrow," she answered, smiling, but not looking at him. Silently he of-fered her his arm, and saw, over her shoulder, that this little scene had not passed unobserved. Two vigilant matrons, in the room behind, were dis-cussing him already; he knew it by the mischiev-ous twinkle of their eyes. He could see, if not hear, his name upon their lips; they had been on the alert for this. What! the secret that he hardly knew himself was, then, an open one. Had he be-trayed it by signs the dullest gossip of them all could read? Curses on their scandalous tongues! He was town-talk unquestionably.

"She knows it, then!" he muttered to himself, as he went out with Sylvia to the carriage. He bade her good-night mechanically.

"Good-night!" she answered, leaning forward to give him her hand. "I shall be at home to-morrow."

Simplest of words! Yet they made his heart leap for joy. Spoken at that moment they were full of significance to him. If the town talked of his love for her, she must not only know it, but have known it long. She must have read his thoughts, have followed, step by step, his mental struggle, appreciating his long forbearance, respecting its motive, tolerating, approving him. And now, that, yielding to the poet's word, he had obeyed his heart, and given all to love, she approved him still. For days he had been her shadow, and she begged for him to-morrow. So, with scarce a word, she had done all a woman could do to make him speak. Yes, it had come to that. Not to tell her would be to wrong her. He must speak now, if only to silence the idle tongues that were busy with her name.

Love is a cruel but an impartial despot; there are no distinctions of rank among his subjects; all are slaves; he laughs at gray hairs and wrinkles; and men have no age when he first bids them hope. The rapture of that moment is like the joy of anticipation, overmastering children, — feverish, irrational, so keen as to be but one remove from pain. It filled Luxmore's heart now; as the fragrance of her roses filled his dreary lodgings. He was living out a short Arabian night. He had made, in very truth, "the receipt of reason a limbec only." Its fumes intoxicated him; through their rosy clouds a sweet, ideal form drew nearer. How should he know that these radiant colors were the colors of his fancy, that he had painted with them a being too lovely for the earth? How should he dream that he was dreaming?

The roses he carried her were sweeter than hers, she said. She held them while she talked, bending over them lovingly. His opportunity had come. His senses had grown strangely acute, so that every small detail of time and place impressed itself upon them. The clear, still, winter afternoon was slowly darkening; there had been a fresh fall of snow, and from the street came up a continuous sound of sleigh-bells. He knew the room by heart; half the things in it were precious heirlooms. She sat between the firelight and the daylight, under a splendid picture that shone down upon her from the wall, — the portrait of an ancestor, a man in the prime of life, handsome and stately, with a faint smile on his shaven lips. In spite of that the face was not agreeable; its fixed look had an air of mockery not at all like hers. Yet so far as the features went, Sylvia bore a strong resemblance to this masterpiece which Luxmore had often admired.

He saw the likeness now, and it made him falter. The old obstacle too loomed up once more. She was so rich. What had he to offer her? He could not hear his own words, as he blundered into a tale, invented on the spur of the moment. A friend had written to him for advice. The man loved, it appeared; that his love was returned, he had grounds for belief, — insufficient ones, perhaps; he feared that sometimes; sometimes, for other reasons, he doubted his right to love her. Meanwhile the world made sport of them. There was, unhappily, no doubt of that. What advice should be

given such a man? Should he be urged to speak
prematurely, and run the risk of losing her; or to
hold his peace, enduring the trying situation as
best he might, forcing her at length to end it, in
one way or the other, by some further sign?

His voice trembled; his speech was hurried, almost incoherent. The girl's cheeks grew pale under it. Two burning spots of color came and went
in them. She understood, of course; the trick was
most transparent; he could not prolong it. He
stopped short, waiting for her answer.

There was a dead silence. Miss Belknap only
lifted the roses to her face, and let them fall again.

"Well," he said, "what is your opinion?"

"I think that he should speak," she answered in
a low voice; "and let it be decided."

"Then he will speak," said Luxmore, firmly.
"The case was mine. I love you."

"You? You—love me?" she asked in a tone
of great surprise.

"Yes; as you have seen—as all the world
knows—I have loved you for months."

"For months? Then why have you never
spoken?"

"Why?" he repeated. What did she mean by
that? Surely she must have known.

"Because—I could not," he continued. "And
yet you understood. Your face just now confirmed
it. You read between my words. You did not
need to be told that they referred to me."

"That is a mistake," she replied slowly. "Until the last moment I did not understand you."

Luxmore had risen and was staring at her now in speechless wonder. Her eyes met his, then looked another way. He did not believe her; she understood that perfectly.

"I was all wrong," she explained. "I thought that it could go on always; that we could always be good friends."

"Is that all?" he demanded huskily. "You do not love me; you cannot love me?"

She shook her head. "I have a great regard for you, — no more than that."

The words made him shiver. He remembered her use of them at their first meeting, and his own thought about them afterward.

"It is the first time I have ever told a woman that I loved her," he returned quietly, "and it will be the last. I have no more to say."

"Do not make me unhappy, Mr. Luxmore," she said, rising to detain him, and now, at last, laying down his roses. "Let me believe that we may meet later with no ill-will, — even as friends."

"And talk of what? The weather? We shall never meet, I hope."

"Don't say so."

"I must say so. Unless — unless — Once more! You cannot love me?"

"No! I am much to blame —"

"I have not blamed you."

"I blame myself. I ought to have known better. I did this once before."

Luxmore recoiled with an angry gesture. "Ah!" he whispered fiercely, "Selden!"

"Did he say so?"

"Not he; you have said it."

She met his look calmly now, standing before him with hands gently clasped. The day's last gleam of sunshine fell upon her, lighting up her golden hair. How fine and soft it was! Her face expressed mingled amazement and vexation at his taking this annoying circumstance so seriously. There was mild compassion in it too, — merely that, no more. Her self-possession maddened him. Her eyes were tearless, hard and clear as the eyes of a Dresden shepherdess; into his own there came a mist through which he saw her less and less distinctly; but, above her head, he could still see the ancestral portrait with its mocking smile.

"You will hate me all your life for this," she said and sighed.

His brows contracted with a look of pain that even she remembered long.

"No," he answered. "I wish that I could hate you."

Then he left her.

III.

It was in the following autumn that Luxmore's "Circe and Ulysses," — his first great picture, — made him suddenly famous. Long before the summer there came rumors that he was bent, at last, upon that higher flight from which his self-distrust had hitherto deterred him. The world saw less of him than of old. And though he looked pale and worn, his air of hopeful determination showed that he was dealing with a problem which hard work would solve. Mordaunt and one or two other friends saw the work in progress and promised great things. Great things, therefore, were expected. And the result, given to the public, surpassed expectation.

He had chosen the moment of the king's first meeting with the enchantress, when, armed with the sprig of moly, he draws his sword defiantly, declining to become a brute at her command. The figures, of life-size, were superbly modelled ; the composition was original and fine, the color fully worthy of it. His triumph proved in every way complete. An English amateur pounced upon the picture, paying without a murmur the sum he demanded for it, carrying it off to London. Hard upon this followed an order for a pendant at his own price. His long apprenticeship had not been served in vain. His reputation rose at last; he had but to sustain the bubble, now soaring into sight of all the world.

From misfortune, fortune. There can be no doubt that to what, in technical phrase, may be termed heart-failure Luxmore's first success was due. In that memorable winter twilight he had broken down utterly at the sight of Sylvia's roses still surviving the desolation of his home. Home! He had hoped for one, and the echo of that hope, resounding in the lonely place, brought him hours of anguish, — days and nights of it, scoring themselves like years. For age is measured more by lost illusions than by actual flight of time. One or two intimate friends saw the change in him and remarked upon it; but they invited no confidences, and he made none. He met the world's glance without flinching, walked erect with a firm step, hugging to himself his "gnarling sorrow" as bravely as the Spartan. Mordaunt alone suspected the truth; but even to him it remained always a mere suspicion. He became, none the less, a model of discreet and devoted friendship. Various were the devices he employed to change the current of his comrade's thoughts, to shorten his hours of solitude. He would break in upon them with some new joke or some new project, carry Luxmore off by force to dine at his table, cheer him there in a hundred ways. But even this kindness had the power to wound. At times Luxmore found the happiness of the house almost unendurable; the children's laughter wrung his heart. Then Mordaunt, seeing this, but failing to comprehend it, would ascribe it to some other cause, and mutter, " What have I said or done to hurt him ? "

The stupor slowly wore itself away, to be succeeded by a fierce reaction. An hour came when Luxmore woke and said: " She has ruined one man ; she shall be the making of another. I cannot hate her. I will forget her. I am not like Selden." He plunged into work, wearily enough at first. Day by day, however, gaining strength from this healthful stimulus, he applied himself more closely, grew more and more at one with his difficult task, found to his delight that something better than his old self had taken possession of him. This it was to live ; no earthly joy that he had ever known was comparable to it. Leaving noble work behind them, men were more than men. And if not the fulfilment, the endeavor ; to that end men were endowed with souls, — " to strive, to seek, to find, and not to yield."

The last fumes of the alembic had cleared away. He knew now that they had lent their colors to an air-drawn shape, a creature of his own mind, totally unreal, perhaps too perfect for material existence. That lovely soul, divine in its perceptions, could never consciously or unconsciously have so betrayed two men ; for her there would have been no second victim to dismiss with an allusion to the first. She

would have been unselfish and considerate, quick
to interpret a silence that every look and every act
of his had contradicted, eager to avert the merest
possibility of danger. With all the weakness of
her sex she would have proved herself the strong-
est and noblest of women, — an angel with a human
heart, not a cold abstraction. How well he remembered Mordaunt's warning, when he had fa-
tally disregarded it. She had only to reveal herself,
to bring home to him the cleverness of that
description.

And yet he could not hate her. When they met,
as sometimes they were forced to meet, passing
each other with a smile of studied cordiality, his
feeling was still one of tenderness toward this
woman whose outward self had dazzled him, whose
inner self he had misconceived. His embodiment
of all gentleness had never been ; by her own
showing that was clearly proved. Yet she came
very near to it ; and in her presence something of
the old glamour returned for a moment to bewilder
him again. Only for a moment, — in the next he
could laugh as men do at the wild hopes of boy-
hood, knowing them to be follies, glad to have
outgrown them. He had other aims now, higher
ones, — far better worth attaining, more glorious
in their rewards. Had she loved him he must one
day have found her out. Then the charm would
have been more rudely broken, the gossamer thread
would have turned into a chain. Her coldness had

saved him, had made a man of him. From the flint had come the spark of fire. All was better as it was.

He often wondered what he should say to her, if by some mischance they were brought into close companionship under too curious eyes. The weather, past, present, and to come, would soon exhaust itself. The numerals were left. He would count, *con espressione*, from one to a hundred, like the tired diner-out of the tale, and request her to do the same. The dreadful infliction must be avoided, if possible; fortunately it was unlikely to occur. He saw so little of the world's people now. Even Mrs. Shirley Allerton had ceased to tax him with neglect. The painter of the " Circe " had justified himself; he was a privileged person with other weighty work on hand, free to come and go as he liked, always sure of a welcome when he wanted it. So, for a long while, the steel encountered the flint only in the open air or in some great assemblage where the law of natural selection prevailed. The two were no longer talked about. Their little affair had been a nine days' wonder at best, and another soon supplanted it. There is no cure for gossip like starvation.

The intercourse still remained one of looks and smiles, when there came an urgent letter from Luxmore's patron calling him to London. Important commissions were said to await him; others in train would surely follow; they needed but his presence. He did not think twice, and deciding not only to go, but to stay indefinitely, began his preparations forthwith. The news was duly chronicled, and his friend Mrs. Allerton read it with a start in her morning paper.

"Oh, Shirley, this is too bad! Mr. Luxmore is going abroad."

"I heard it last night at the club. I meant to tell you."

"And he never, — at least I suppose he never, — I really must interfere now."

"What on earth are you talking about?"

"Don't be obtuse. Miss Belknap —"

"Oh, that's it! I thought you thought they were not on speaking terms."

"They must speak. I shall ask them to dinner, and make him take her in."

Mr. Allerton laughed. "With another vacant place, I suppose. No, my dear; I won't consent to it."

"But —"

"I will not have him badgered. Let him speak if he chooses; if not —"

"How can he, without an opportunity?"

"You may give him that, if you please; but only that."

"How?"

"Who dines here to-morrow? The Mexican minister?"

"Yes."

6

" Very well ; ask a few of the enlightened to
come in afterward, Jack with them, and his Jill,—
or jilt, which is it ?   But. mind. no compulsion.   Is
it agreed ? "

" Agreed ; yes."

Accordingly on the following night, Luxmore,
talking earnestly with his hostess, looked up and
found that he had been led into a corner where
Miss Belknap stood alone.   She put out her hand
appealingly.   He was forced to take it ; and he had
no sooner done so than Mrs. Allerton disappeared
as if by magic.   The rooms were large, the company was small.   For a moment they stood silent,
face to face, almost as far from the Mexican minister as he from Mexico.

" I am sorry to hear that you are going away,"
said the voice, once so familiar, now slightly tremulous, as he observed ; he listened closely to his
own, and found no tremor in it.

" Ah !   And why ? " he asked.

" I do not like to think that an American wil-
lingly gives up his native land."

He smiled somewhat scornfully.   " A great philosopher once said, ' Let no man call himself an
Athenian or a Corinthian, but a citizen of the
world.'   You have studied the philosophers.   Is
not that good advice ? "

" You did not think so once."

" No.   But we grow wiser as we grow older.
I have learned my lesson in philosophy."

A faint color came into her face. She studied her fan attentively, opening and shutting it, stroking its feathers with the caressing gesture that he remembered.

"Won't you sit down?" she asked.

There was a small sofa near them, under a bust of Plato. Wondering a little at his own indifference, Luxmore took his seat there at her side.

"I have seen your picture," she continued. "It is very fine. I have wished to add my word to the others."

"Thank you," he replied. "One does what one can, and is none the worse, I hope, for recognition."

"That is a pleasure of which you are depriving us. Art here struggles for existence; it needs the help of every skilful hand, and yours is turned against it. Stay; it is your duty."

"One's first duty is to one's self. I go where I can work to the best advantage."

"I see. Your work absorbs you; you have no other end in life."

"None."

"And does it make you happy?"

"I do not ask so much of it. I have lost a hope, but I have gained a virtue, — the virtue of contentment. In this life we are all servants and not masters; the rewards come after. I serve to win them. I live only for a few letters in high relief upon a tombstone, — for a statue, perhaps; for fame, immortality, who knows? for happiness elsewhere."

He looked not at her, but straight before him, through the half-empty rooms, toward the Mexican minister who had just risen to take leave. A star glittered upon his breast. The light of it flashed in Luxmore's eyes.

At a slight sound beside him he turned his head. One of the slender sticks of her fan had broken in Miss Belknap's hands. "It is nothing," she said, rising. "As you were saying, you have grown older, if not wiser. All your ideas are completely changed."

He rose too. "No," he said. "My ideal,— that is all."

"And nothing can change that?"

"Nothing in this world."

She held out her hand once more. "Since you will go, then, I wish you all possible success."

"It is to you that I shall owe it," he replied, looking at her now, as their hands clasped. He could hardly believe his own eyes, for hers were full of tears.

"They are going," he said. "Shall I take you to our hostess?"

"No. I shall stay a little longer. Good-night."

"Good-night,— until we meet again!"

On his way home he reviewed their talk lightly, laughing to himself. "And yet," he thought, "she would have flung me over. I would not have

trusted her even then." That was his conclusion.
To his last hour he will never doubt it.

"Until we meet again!" We toss a ball into
the air for chance to catch, to return or not, at
pleasure. In this case it was returned, but only
after twenty years, throughout which Luxmore remained true to his ideal, winning honors, orders,
stars as brilliant as the Mexican's. The better to
enjoy them he went through the form of deniza-
tion, and became a British subject. He grew gray
and rich and stout and comfortable, — but alone.
He never married.

One night, at a private view, his name was on
everybody's lips. His picture had been pronounced
by acclamation the picture of the year. The galleries were thronged. Luxmore had offered his
arm to a stately dowager, and as they made their
way about she caught the whisper of his name, and
wondered that he did not seem to hear it.

"How I envy you," she said.

He laughed. "Envy me? Why?"

"You are Luxmore. That's all. Who is the
old, young person coming this way? Do I know
her?"

The figure passed on in the crowd and was gone;
but not before Luxmore recognized the face and
returned its cordial greeting with a smile.

"No; she looked at you," his companion rattled
on. "The eyes are fine; but she makes me think
of a faded leaf. Who is she, pray?"

"An American," said Luxmore. "I knew her once, slightly. I am not sure about the name."

Later on he informed himself that she was called Miss Belknap. She too had never married. But she had left the gallery. They did not meet again.

That same night an acquaintance stopped him in the club, to speak of a brother painter who had lately died.

"I have just heard the news. Onslow is to have a niche in the crypt of St. Paul's. Jolly good thing, is n't it? I wonder if he knows."

"I hope not," said Luxmore. "Was that the best they could do?"

The man stared and went away. Luxmore, left to himself, sighed heavily.

"The crypt of St. Paul's! I wish it were I instead of Onslow." Then his thought took another turn. "After all, I am Luxmore," he said with a smile. And wheeling his chair a little nearer to the fire, he took a cat-nap before turning in.

" I T is a bargain, Monsieur, — a bargain ! The rent is a mere nothing ; puisqu'il y a du confort ici," said the old concierge, as he threw open one of the shutters, and flooded the room with dusty sunshine.

The apartment was *au premier*, at the back of a small court numbered 59 of the Rue Neuve St. Augustin. No. 59, — I give it fearlessly, since even its foundation-stones have long been Haussmannized away.

The court was flooded with sunshine that was not dusty, and a great plane-tree grew in one corner, close against an ivy-covered wall. The yellow placard, " À LOUER," hanging at the door, had been the bait luring me into this mouse-trap, as it certainly proved to be.

But all that comes later on. For the present it is enough to say that the room was comfortably furnished after the old Venetian manner, and hung with Cordova leather, old too, and real ; beyond, there was a salon, with a floor so highly polished that I narrowly escaped a sprained ankle in crossing it ; and a chamber, commonplace enough but for the chintz hangings with which its walls and

ceiling were draped oppressively in wide plaits
that met overhead in a central rosette, somehow
suggesting the interior decoration of a coffin.   In
spite of this untimely thought, and of the su-
perfluous *antichambre* and *salle-à-manger*, useless
incumbrances in bachelor quarters, I took the
apartment for a month, to the evident delight
of old Casimir, whose feather-duster twitched
expressively in his palsied hand.

The tremulous eagerness of this good gentleman
made me half suspect that he had not the remotest
right to let the rooms at all.   But he told a
well-varnished tale of an old proprietor who hated
women, and who passed his life in search of a
country so civilized as to do without them.   From
this journey of desperation he returned now and
then to restore his tired senses in the coffined
chamber, and to gather courage for a new departure.   It was midsummer ; I might keep the rooms
until the autumn, — not an hour longer, since the
patron would then be likely to pounce down upon
his possessions, unannounced, at any moment.
Just now, he was believed to be in Lapland.

When I moved in, that very afternoon, a guilty
feeling of intrusion overcame me.   The place was
so luxurious, so well ordered, so unlike the four
walls of lodging for which one pays.   In the
library of the leather hangings the patron's books
were upon the shelves ; his portfolio, his paper-
knife upon the table ; the ink in the miniature

helmet of blue steel was dry, it is true ; but there
lay the well-worn quill beside it. " The room re-
veals the man," says Diderot ; granting this, the
patron was a man of taste and well informed. I
took down some of the books ; here were superb
bindings, old and rare editions. Upon one fly-leaf
his name was written, — Marius Morizot, — the
hand clear and fine, like a woman's. Casimir
had said that he was old. Bibliophile and traveller, with the means to follow his fantastic bent,
this patron would certainly be an agreeable man
to meet on his own ground ; that is, if one came
properly introduced. All here was as if he had
left it yesterday. What if the door were to open
and admit him at the next moment ?

Just then the door did open, but only Casimir
came in, bringing firewood ; for the sun had
already left the little court in shadow, and there
was an unseasonable chill in the waning summer
day. The old man wore a black skull-cap over
his thin, gray hair, and a green baize apron that
swathed him nearly to the ankles. He chattered
about the fire as he built and lighted it ; all
the time holding under his arm the eternal feather-
duster, which seemed to be his badge of office.
I had lately seen, at the Comédie Française, Reg-
nier's masterpiece, the sly old servant in " La joie
fait peur," — the picture of amiable senility. Here
was the thing itself.

" The patron has his treasures," I said, stroking

tenderly the crushed levant that enshrined a numbered reprint of André Chénier.

Casimir looked at the shelves with a certain
respect, and then shrugged his shoulders.

" Yes, but not there," he answered.

Thinking that he referred to the glittering objects of the salon, I treated myself to a complacent
smile, as I quietly put up the book.

" Not there," he repeated, shuffling toward me
in his loose slippers, and letting his voice die
away into the important whisper that is the em-
phasis of a French man-of-all-work. " Ah, if
Monsieur knew ! "

" Knew what ? " I asked. " Have we a gold
mine at our feet ? "

He chuckled and nodded. " Better than that,
Monsieur. See ! "

Then he pushed aside one of the hangings, and
showed me that it covered a door of burnished
steel.

" A safe ? "

" Yes, Monsieur, in the wall."

" And of such size ! " I continued ; for the door-
way, though narrow, was higher than my head.
" What can he keep there ? "

" Jewels, Monsieur," said Casimir, enjoying my
surprise. " Jewels from the ends of the earth
laid away in little drawers lined with velvet as
soft as the down of a bird. It is a passion with
him ; the collection is a property in itself."

I laid my hand gently upon the shining metal ;
it might have been the door of a tomb. I drew
back, shivering. The thought of these untold
riches, hardly out of reach, disturbed me ; I felt
in a measure responsible for their safety.

" The door is locked, of course," said I.

" Oh, yes, Monsieur ; only the patron has the
key." He brushed the door lightly with his
feather-tips, as though he were dealing with some
fragile work of art, and then dropped the curtain
over it.

" Casimir ! You have your master's leave to
let these rooms ; you are sure ? "

" Oh, certainly, Monsieur ; Monsieur need give
himself no uneasiness, it is permitted at this
season. In the summer-time Monsieur Morizot
always absents himself. He has been nearly two
years away."

I changed the subject, though I doubted him
instinctively.

" What is Monsieur Morizot like ? " I asked.

" A lamb, Monsieur ; amiable, as one cannot
be more so. Monsieur, then, has not remarked
his portrait ? "

The pictures were chiefly modern, and were
none too well lighted ; I had barely glanced at
them. Casimir led me to this one, which hung
in a dark corner, so high that the flame of a
candle held up at arm's length but just revealed
it. The face was long, thin, sharp-featured, and

sallow, with the prevailing moustache and imperial of the time. But the eyes were fine and
friendly. On the whole, I felt happier about Monsieur Morizot. He had the gentle, high-bred look
of that Van Dyck father in the long gallery of
the Louvre.

"And yet he hates women. Was he never
married ? "

" Never, Monsieur ; in youth he had a disappointment, they say, and now it would be somewhat late for him to think again of that. At
his age one no longer makes such plans."

His hand shook more than ever, and the melted
wax of the candle ran over, one drop falling upon
the floor. " He is good, the patron," he murmured, so tenderly that the drop might have been
a tear from his own failing eyes.

When the old retainer had left me, I dismissed
all scruples, and unpacked my trunk in the little
chamber, singing to myself in the happiest of
moods. I was in luck, evidently. Even should
Monsieur Morizot turn up, I felt sure that he
would accept my explanation, supposing one to
be necessary. But he would not come. I doubted
Casimir no longer.

I found in the library an arm-chair covered
with stamped leather like that of the walls ; the
arms supported by hard featured goddesses, —
wood-nymphs, perhaps, — redundant in the matter
of bust, tapering off like terminal figures into

the chair-legs below. Wheeling this up to the table, I sat down awhile to do nothing and devour my brain, as the inhuman proverb puts it. In the gathering twilight the room was almost dark, but I saw it all, or nearly all, over the mantel in a narrow, oblong mirror, there reflected by Casimir's cheerful blaze. The first fire of the season invites contemplation, and my thoughts wandered as fitfully as the mellow light that played about the tarnished gilding of the leather. When I am alone I am apt to grow inconsequent, to a degree that would distress one who makes a labor of thinking.

Hunger is a sharp reminder, and before long I realized that I was hungry. So I hastily pulled myself together, and shutting the door upon my golden walls, strolled up the Boulevard to the Passage des Princes. I dined well at Peter's, opposite the window of innumerable meerschaums, and after dinner, went out by the side gate of the Passage into the Rue Favart. The doors of the Opéra Comique stood invitingly open, and I was tempted to turn toward them, and read the bill of the play, " L'Ombre," of Flotow ; Gounod's " Gallia." In the first, Madame Priola. Lovely Madame Priola, long since forgotten ! Do you live on, to look into your glass and sigh for those dear old days when all Paris adored you ? Or have you made, in truth, your final exit into Père-la-Chaise or Montparnasse, to sleep out there

a longer night than any other you have known ?
To one cruelty of life all a man's experience
can never reconcile him, — that a pretty woman
may not hold her own forever.

I went in, stayed the performance out, and left
the theatre somewhat dashed in spirits ; the echo
of Gounod's solemn music seemed to follow me
like a ghostly footfall under the flaring lights,
by the painted kiosk-windows. The sky was overcast ; a drop or two of rain fell. The great doors
of No. 59 were closed and locked of course ; at
that hour I could have expected nothing else. But
Casimir slept soundly ; it was long before I could
make him hear, though I pulled the bell till the
whole place resounded. The rain came on in
earnest, and I was at the despairing point, when
the door gave a welcome click and swung back
an inch or two. I stumbled in through the darkness, passed the lodge where I could hear Casimir
swearing to himself drowsily without a thought
of challenging me, and guided myself by the hand-
rail of the staircase straight to my own door. I
struck a match, found the key, and went in.

The outer rooms were black and unfriendly ;
through them I saw a thread of light from the
library door to which I groped my way. The
light came from a stately *modérateur* lamp that
stood upon the table, and I blessed Casimir for
his forethought ; but for the lamp, the room,
at the first glance, seemed to be as I had left

it. The carved chair was drawn up before the
fire, which still burned brightly. That I found a
fire and not a heap of ashes, might have struck
me as a curious circumstance, but I set this down
to Casimir's forethought too ; all the more readily
that my clothes were wet and that I needed it
to dry them, as I proceeded to do.

Standing thus before the chimney with the
crackling fagots at my heels, I observed a book
upon the table. It lay close to the arm of the
great chair, — so close, in fact, that one sitting
there could hardly fail to see it even at twilight.
Yet it had escaped my notice until now. What
book ? The moment my unspoken question was
answered, I felt absolutely sure that it had never
before been in my hands. Its vellum covers were
worn and worm-eaten ; its musty leaves were yellow with age. I read the title, " The Trial of
François Ravaillac for the Murder of King Henry
IV. 1610." I could hardly have forgotten that
book had I taken it down.

Immediately a strange terror seized me, —
vague, unreasoning it was, like a child's in the
dark. I dropped the book, caught up a candle,
and peered into the chamber, then searched the
other rooms throughout. I saw no one, heard no
sound. I was alone ; yet this knowledge failed
to reassure me. I spoke and was startled at
my own voice. I tried to sing, but the walls
gave back a mocking echo that was unendurable,

and I returned to the library with the same
childish dread of nothing still oppressing me like
the remembrance of a nightmare.

I can recall distinctly my struggle to conquer
this feeling, and I know that I must have con-
quered it; for I sat down in the arm-chair, and
began to read the trial of Ravaillac, —

"The prisoner is sworn, and asked his name,
age, rank, and place of abode.

"He said that his name was François Ravaillac,
born and dwelling at Angoulême, between thirty-
one and thirty-two years of age."

I can see those lines now, in all their quaintness
of type, as one makes a sun-picture by a sudden
closing of the eyes. I remember that I read on
and on, till I came to a page so stained as to be
indistinct, part of which had been torn away.
Then I must have fallen into a doze, — a mere
cat-nap of a moment only. I woke with a start,
unable, at first, to recognize the surroundings.

The lamp had run down, after the provoking
manner of French *modérateurs*. I knew that it
only needed winding, and leaning over the table, I
gave the key a turn or two, but I was too late;
the lamp went out in a long, smoky trail. Yet
the room was not quite dark; the fire burned on,
flickering at my feet, and making fantastic shadows
in the glass.

In the glass! I looked at it, and grew numb
with horror. For I saw there the reflection of a

man's face, so hideous in its expression that, even
in a crowd, one would have turned from it with
loathing. I have never been able to describe it;
in that uncertain light it had no color, I could
barely trace its outline. But I should know that
face if I saw it at the top of the Great Pyramid, or in
the plains of Arizona, — anywhere, indeed, — upon
the instant; and I should shudder at the sight, as
I do now at the thought, like a frightened animal.

For a few seconds I was helpless. My muscles
refused to act; I could not even turn my head to
look behind me. Thus, with all senses gone but
one, I saw the face drawing nearer to my chair
and looking down at it. The lines grew more
distinct, — a strange mark came out upon the
check as if the skin there had contracted. Then,
with an effort that seemed like a trial of strength
with some force unseen, I caught the arm of the
chair, and springing to my feet, wheeled about
upon the dark, silent spaces of the room, conscious
only of a sudden draught of cold air that chilled
me to the bone.

Darkness, there was nothing else. Yet I turned
again to the glass, finding only my own figure,
scarcely recognizable. Then for the first time, I
was aware that my left hand, cold and damp like
a dead man's, still clasped the old book, marking
my place between its leaves. I shivered and would
have laid it down; but instead of that, I flung it
from me into the fire with a shriek that set the

room ringing. For the stain upon its torn page had deepened and freshened, and was oozing out upon my fingers, — they were red with it. Kneeling at the hearth I wiped away the drops with my handkerchief, and burned that too.

Still on the hearth I crouched and listened. If there were only something human to face and challenge! Not a sound. But again the current of cold air, as if from an open door or window. That, at least, was real. I found my candle, lighted it at the fire, and searched the room once more. To my great surprise I discovered in the darkest corner a small door that I had never seen, — one of those blind doors so common in French apartments, cunningly contrived to fit a panel of the wall. It stood ajar, moreover, as though forced open by some mischievous gust of the night-wind that had lost its way in the house and then made a frantic effort to get out again. Rejoiced to account so easily for one disturbing element at least, I pushed the door aside, and saw merely a narrow, flagged corridor, leading to a servants' stairway communicating with the floor below, — the ground-floor, for the house had no *entresol.* By the dim light I held, I could distinguish three steps leading down into awful blackness, like a murderous oubliette of the Middle Ages. I strained my eyes and listened. There was nothing more to be seen, but my ears caught a faint sound, startling at that hour, though by day I should have laughed at it, — simply the noise of running water gently falling, as if from a pipe, upon the pavement below. I went on cautiously to the stair-rail, leaned over it, and looked down. No one; but under the stairs in the dark the water went splashing on intermittently, as though it fell first upon invisible hands, — washing them, perhaps. The thought suggested itself instantly.

"Who is there?" I shouted, lowering the light toward the dark corner, but in vain.

The water stopped. There was no other answer.

"Who is there?" I repeated in a voice that was not mine.

I heard a shuffling step, and there came a blast of the night air strong enough to put out the light, if I had not drawn back, shielding the flame with my hand. A door below me quietly closed, and all was still again.

I rushed down the stairs and found the door. It was securely bolted; the bolts were rusted, — I tried one, and could not stir it.

Then, out in the court, a harsh cry rang back along the walls, "Cordon!" — the familiar call to the sleeping concierge. "Cordon!" the same rough voice repeated. The heavy street-door fell into place with a dull, jarring sound. The presence, whatever it was, had escaped scot-free into the world of Paris.

Drip, drip, behind me I heard the water falling now, drop by drop, upon the stones. There was nothing else to show that I had not been dreaming.

I gave one searching look at the dismal little corner, and then fled from it and from the house forever. In less time than it takes to tell it, I had rushed through the rooms overhead and down again by the main staircase, out into the court and on through the falling rain, shouting to Casimir as I went, " Cordon! cordon! cordon!" I woke echoes there that drove me half mad; I beat upon the door. At last the cord was drawn, and I found myself in the street, where I recovered my senses sufficiently to put on my hat and coat, snatched up in my flight, mechanically, from the table in the *antichambre.*

I went back to my hotel, and passed a night to which that uneasy one of Clarence was as nothing. In the morning, very early, I hurried out again, laughing at my folly. The day was fine and bright, as only Paris can be; and yet I trembled upon turning into the court, where, however, I found nothing more terrible than Casimir, watering his flowers and talking to a gray cat that rubbed itself affectionately against his shins. The old man started when he saw me, and looked from me to the window behind which he supposed I had been sleeping.

" Monsieur rises early," said he.

" Yes. I am called away. You will be kind enough to pack my trunk and send it after me."

" Monsieur gives up the rooms?"

" Unavoidably. It does not matter; they are paid for, all the same."

Surprise made him speechless for a moment. The cat came slowly toward me, purring. I stooped and stroked it between the ears.

" He is called Chambord, Monsieur; he lives upon raw meat, but he is very kind and gentle. I regret that Monsieur goes away."

" Thank you. Casimir, what strange man was in the house last night ? "

" Monsieur, I do not understand. There was no one."

" You let no one out, then ? "

" Oh, that, of course. The house has many apartments, many lodgers. I do not count them in my sleep."

" Nevertheless," I said with some warmth, " there was a stranger in my rooms last night. I saw him."

" Monsieur was dreaming. It is impossible."

" But I can describe him to you." And I tried to do so, making only a stammering failure of it.

Casimir shrugged his shoulders.

Then I remembered the curious mark upon the man's cheek, and put in that evidence triumphantly.

The dull eyes opened a little wider; but he smiled and shook his head.

" *Sapristi!* Now I know that Monsieur was surely dreaming. That is the Brazilian, Cornelio, the good patron's *valet de chambre.*"

" Well, then, I tell you he has come back."

" But, Monsieur — "

" I swear it to you."

" Impossible. Monsieur Morizot keeps him always at his side. They are both in Lapland."

I argued with him to no purpose. He grew angry, and in his excitement, tipped over his watering-pot upon Chambord, who turned tail and disappeared. I could convince him of nothing but my own imbecility; and so I left him, muttering strange oaths among his flowers.

One rarely fails to recall a startling bit of his own experience the first time its date comes round again. So it happened that this adventure was uppermost in my mind one midsummer night of the following year, on board the good steamer " Baron Osy," bound from London to Antwerp. We had left the White Tower just at noon, and had dropped leisurely down the overburdened Thames, threading our cautious way through larger and smaller ocean craft, in and out among tow-boats and barges, and awkward little luggers with red sails and spankers; past the big guns of Woolwich, and Greenwich Hospital with its white-haired veterans, whose reckoning leaves off where ours begins; by Tilbury Fort and Gravesend, where the great river, broadened to an estuary, stretches out its arms to greet the Medway and the two go wandering off here and there in a tangle of green hills that know no winter but are always green. So we had come out into yellower and wilder water; the sun had set in a bank of cool, gray clouds; the white cliffs and glimmering lights of Margate were already low on the horizon; and the long twilight crept down upon us slowly, imperceptibly.

I had seen but few passengers, all of the heaviest and most uninteresting modern Flemish pattern; but a chance remark of one of the stewards led me to think that there were others of consequence, holding themselves aloof in their cabins. One by one, those who were about me on the after-deck had gone below as the night-breeze strengthened. I knew that the stars were coming out, that under the pale-green streak of western sky the English coast was fast receding; but my thoughts were hundreds of miles away. With them I was really strolling through the Passage des Princes and back along the Boulevard, humming as I walked the doctor's air in " L'Ombre," —

> " Midi, minuit!
> Le jour, la nuit !
> Midi, c'est la vie,
> Minuit, la mort — oui ! "

And so on, through all the details of that troubled night. I lived again in Monsieur Morizot's apartment; I saw his chair at the fire, his book upon the table; nay, even the old letter-press danced before my eyes, —

" The prisoner is sworn, and asked his name, age, rank, and place of abode.

" He said that his name was François Ravaillac, born and dwelling at Angoulême — "

The sound of my voice brought me back to the deck of the " Baron Osy." I had spoken the words aloud. I turned and saw that they must have been overheard by a passenger who stood at the rail, not ten feet away. He wore a close-fitting, pointed cap and a long dark coat, buttoned tightly under his chin, and these garments had a suggestive richness in them. A splendid jewel too shone upon his hand. But his eyes were fixed on me with a look in which fear and wonder mingled strangely ; his face seemed white as death, — and it was the face of the valet, Cornelio.

I realized an unknown power in the words which I had spoken ; and without moving from my place I finished the broken sentence from the trial of Ravaillac, then repeated it word for word from the beginning. With that, the mark upon his cheek quivered convulsively ; he gave a wild cry, like some brute brought to bay, and with one appealing look, as if toward imaginary pursuers closing in upon him, he flung himself over the rail into the sea.

I rushed to the ship's side as one of the hands, who had seen him jump, tore a life-preserver from the guards, and threw it after him. We caught sight of an arm tossed up in the foaming wake

far behind; a wave swept over it. The engines
were stopped, and a boat was lowered; after
a long time it came back, bringing only the wet
corks. The old gray sexton of the sea works
quickly and well.

We found his name registered upon the list, —
Ramon Quizás, *rentier*, of Rio. He had no companion, and his trunks were stored somewhere
on the quay at Antwerp. When I left the city
they still remained there unclaimed.

Three years later, in one of the continental
reading-rooms, I took up the " Figaro," to divert
myself with its *faits divers* and *échos de Paris*.
Between the last *mot* of Madame X., and the
announcement of a fête at Asnières, I found a
line of reference to a matter familiar enough, as
it seemed, to all but casual readers; namely, the
division among the heirs-at-law of a handsome property, — that of one Monsieur Morizot. The name,
and the mysterious importance given it, roused my
curiosity, and I wrote at once to a Parisian crony
for fuller information. This was his answer : —

" Have you retired from the world, that you cease
to read the news of it? We are worn out with
details of the life and death of Monsieur Morizot.
Pardon me, then, if I recite them to you very briefly.
The worthy man lived, *en garçon*, in one of those
houses of the Rue Neuve St. Augustin already condemned to make way for the new avenue which will

be a marvel. Like you he was a traveller, and he often remained for years an absentee, staying away at last longer than the code allows. He became to all intents and purposes a dead man, and his heirs demanded to share his estate, and to break up his collection of jewels, known to be of great value. Man proposes! The safe was opened, but it had been rifled, *mon ami.* They found there, instead, the owner's body, stabbed through and through. The good soul had made a hard fight of it. His hand still clutched a bit of watch-chain, identified as the property of a certain Brazilian ape of a servant who never left him. Our *haute police* is enormously cunning. Bit by bit, the case has been worked up, and this is what happened. The two arrived late one night at the Northern Railway station, where, to save time, at the servant's suggestion, their trunks were left to be claimed in the morning. Thus they installed themselves at home without stir and unan-nounced. Then the man got the better of his master, and became in his turn an absentee. No one ever dreamed of the arrival or the departure, yet now it is all clear as though we saw it in a glass, — the very date proved by the fragment of a journal found in the pocket of what was once Monsieur Morizot. Heed the warning, and travel no more ; but marry, and let madame watch over you. Get thee a wife, *mon amour! Et voilà tout!*"

I answered my foreign correspondent in good American fashion, by asking a question. Upon what date, I prayed him, was the crime committed ? His reply brought me a printed slip, fixing upon the very night of my adventure, *but in the year preceding it*. And on this point all known records of the affair obstinately agree.

That Señor Ramon Quizás and the valet, Cornelio, were one and the same, I have no manner of doubt ; but that he ever could have revisited the scene of his double crime is inconceivable. Whose face, then, appeared to me in the mirror ? Whose hands were washed in the running water ? Who, besides myself, clamored there in the dark for release from his own haunting fears ? Did I, by some strange coincidence, dream these things, one after another in quick succession ? Or did the murderer leave behind him in his flight a ghostly presence, to play his hideous part out, time and time again, while the faithful glass of Venice reflected line for line, moment for moment ? I cannot answer. But now, when I walk in the Avenue de l'Opéra, I am grateful even for that dullest of improvement's dull marches, sweeping, as it does, all memory but mine of my grim lodging from the face of the earth.

THE TINCTURE OF SUCCESS.

A S Hazard read the last words of the manuscript, Purkitt knocked the ashes from his
long clay pipe and looked up with a cheerful smile.
Cheerfulness, however, was the main characteristic
of his somewhat puffy little personality; and on
that unwrinkled forty-five-year-old face, rendered
rosier than usual to-night by frequent draughts of
gin-and-water, a smile had no more promise in it
to anxious eyes than has a morning rainbow.

" Well ? " said the other, faintly.

He was a man under thirty; but time had kept
him in mind evidently. Already he looked old.
His face was thin, pale, and worn; at first sight of
it one might well have wondered when he had last
eaten a good dinner, and what his next meal was
likely to be.

" Well," returned Purkitt, irresolutely. Then,
after a moment, " I think your style is charming."

Hazard tossed down his work with a show of
carelessness ; but one sheet of it fell from the
table upon the dusty floor, and he picked this up,
to brush it with his coat-sleeve before replying.

" Thank you, Dick ! " said he. " I see ; it is a
failure."

Dick Purkitt pushed forward his empty glass and twirled it about with finger-tips unmarred by any deformity of labor. They had toiled early and late, but only with the pen.

"Victor, dear boy, you did not expect me to call the tale a work of genius, worthy of — well, say Yarrow, did you?"

"No, Dick, of course not. But I did hope to show a bit of progress; perhaps, even, to stir your British public up a little. I worked so hard; and they will no more be stirred by it than that old duffer in the corner there."

Speaking thus, with eyes that in vain strove not to glisten, he indicated a man whom they had found asleep by the gray embers of the tavern-fire. Dick studied for a moment the drooping figure, with its folded arms and hat drawn down over the eyes in deep, serene unconsciousness, still the same.

"He has not turned a hair," said he. "Yes; the British public is like that. You must strike a higher note to rouse it. And yet the story is a good story; not Yarrow, but still —"

"Yarrow — always Yarrow!"

"Dear boy, have patience. Even Yarrow had to learn his letters. Look at me! Grinding the mill for five-and-twenty years, and still at it, — a hack writer on the 'Tavistock Review.'"

"Yes, but —" Hazard stopped and sighed.

"I know. You want to tell me your art is different. That is true, and I honor you for it. I keep the beaten path, and you must climb. Even now, I could not begin to do that thing of yours. Send it to the magazines."

" The magazines ! " echoed Hazard, bitterly.

" Well, magazine, then. You 're too sensitive ; that 's one of your troubles. Shall I tell you another ? Your work is imitative, — far too suggestive of your master, who is Yarrow, I say, whether you like it or not. Give him the cold shoulder. You are young, but you have lived. Take some passage of your life, and put your heart into it. If it hurts you, so much the better. The public is as cruel as a Vestal virgin. I tell you, it wants blood. Where did you dine to-day ? "

" Here, in the Silver Cross. Jugged hare and apple-tart, — not a bad dinner for one-and-three-pence. It 's the best luncheon-bar I know in London."

" I thought you looked hungry ; so am I — as a horse. I say, bring us supper, will you ? Cold joint, and plenty of it, — the best cheese you 've got. Beer for this gentleman, and gin for me. As you say, Hazard, one lives well here for Fleet Street. *Per me*, I prefer the Bristol. For Heaven's sake, William, coax that fire up with another coal or two. Don't you know it 's snowing outside ? Now then, Hazard, here 's the beef. Pitch right in, — that 's American, is n't it ? Show your Yankee spirit, and make victory of defeat, as you did at

Bunker's Hill. Damn it, man, Victor is your name!"

All this stir in the little back parlor at last roused its third occupant, who stretched his legs, yawned, and growled, then rose, buttoned his heavy dark coat about him, and thrust his hands into the pockets; finally, with a nod to Purkitt, he passed into the bar, mumbling to himself, inaudibly, as he went. They heard him shuffle on to the street-door and go out.

Hazard had looked for an instant at his dark face, deeply furrowed, with an iron-gray moustache large enough to cover the lips and half the military tuft upon the chin; with enormous eyebrows, black as jet, under which the eyes shrunk away into what seemed empty sockets; yet in them lurked a scrutiny so keen that the boy had lowered his own eyes at once, catching his breath with something like a chill. The jar of the closing door was a relief.

"Who is that man?" he asked.

"His name is Rose," said Purkitt. "Odd chap, is n't he? Some men like him; I don't, or I would have asked him to stay. Queer devil, — they tell absurd stories of him."

"What stories?"

"Oh, mere rot. They say he dabbles in the black arts, the occult and the unknowable. He may deal with the Devil, for aught I know; there are various ways of doing that, and his looks are in favor of him. But the rest is rubbish."

" What is the rest ?   Go on."

" Well, that he can live forever, if he pleases. That he pursues the philosopher's stone, and has caught up with the elixir of long life; that he is one of those German fellows, — a Rosicrucian.   He is shy about stating his age, and his name happens to be Rose.   That's all, but it's quite enough to start the story."

" Has he no profession ? "

" Yes, a capital profession.   He is an inventor who has never invented anything ; with means, of course, or he couldn't exist.   Drake said, the other day, he had seen his rooms ; but there was nothing in them, so far as I could discover.   Eat your supper, old man, and let us change the subject.   I hate quackery and all its works."

They ate and drank until a late hour, — that is, one made a good meal, and the other did the drinking.   Gin agreed with him, he said, and he seemed none the worse for it.   As they parted, the barmaid complimented him on his good looks, he retorting in a way that led her to blush.   For a time the place rang with his boisterous mirth, and when he was gone the girl sighed, and told William that Mr. Purkitt was a nice gentleman.

Victor Hazard would have confirmed her statement, had it been made in his hearing.   Purkitt took his arm and returned good advice for it, as they splashed up Fleet Street to the Strand through the wet snow-flakes, melting into grimy mud at their feet.

"Now, dear boy, do as I tell you. Send that thing off to-morrow morning, and begin on another the moment you leave the bank. Strike deep; stick the knife in up to the handle, and turn it round. Don't give way, whatever happens. Fight the good fight, and win. And if you get short, mind you come to me."

"Yes, Dick," said Hazard. There was something in his throat that choked off further speech; so he merely stood still, to detach himself from the friendly arm and offer his hand instead. "Good-night to you!"

"To be sure, there is the bridge; you go that way. Well, good-night! God bless you!"

And Purkitt went sliding on over another mile of the slippery pavement to his club, in Piccadilly, where other dear boys were gathered about the fire, and where he made a cheerful night of it, putting the struggles and possible successes of the young Anglo-American quite out of mind.

Hazard waited on the corner looking after his friend. His throat no longer troubled him; the tears trickled down his cheeks.

"What a good fellow!" he thought; "and how little of me he really knows! He has never had to worry about his bread-and-butter; he cannot imagine what it is."

Across the way he heard a sudden slamming of doors; and then a laughing crowd burst out upon him. The play was over at the Lyceum Theatre.

8

The cabbies swore and shouted and lashed their
patient horses. A young girl, all in white, gleamed
like a will-o'-the-wisp under the columns of the
portico and disappeared. Hazard, turning away,
walked on to the gate of Waterloo Bridge, paid the
moderate price of solitude, and speedily it was his.
Half-way over he stopped to look down. The
sluggish river below crept on darkly in the night,
lapping filth and squalor, and nameless horrors almost inconceivable, to purify itself at last in the
healing water of the sea. Above him too there
was little more than darkness; the distant lights
blinked feebly, softened by the snow. All looked
solemn, mysterious, death-like. It was the place
of suicides, — the very time of year, as the historian of statistics demonstrated long ago. Hazard
smiled at it.

"There is always this," he muttered, fixing his
eyes upon a single flake of snow that passed
through the narrow circle illumined by the nearest
bridge-lamp and then vanished. "Always this to
help us out. A snow-flake on the river in the
night, — gone before it strikes the water, — it leaves
no mark. How can a thread of talent hope to do
more upon the black indifference of the world?"
He leaned over the parapet, and drew back.
"Not yet!" he said and went his way resolutely,
defiantly.

He lived in one of those attic chambers on the
Surrey shore over which a loop of railway de-

scribes the wide arc of a circle between Cannon
Street and Charing Cross. This ten-minute journey, with its dissolving views of the river, the Em-
bankment, the towering landmarks of Westminster
and Ludgate Hill, is one of the sights of London ;
one that wears well too, and may be seen many
times before the dull lens of habit blurs it. Its
best side was all at Hazard's command. The out-
look from his window over the sooty tiles, from
the Victoria Tower on one side to the dome of St.
Paul's on the other, was never twice the same.
The fogs in winter did their black and yellow
worst, but they were forever shifting, — strange
lights shone out in them ; and at night they were
almost sure to lift and let the stars look down.
The trains thundered about his ears incessantly,
but a noise that lasts is no longer a nuisance ; only
silence becomes painful, — as on a steamship when
the engine stops in mid-ocean, and one longs for
the beating soul of the machine.

Victor Hazard was the son of a poor gentleman
who had pinched himself to give his boy what he
considered a suitable education ; then, dying suddenly, had left him alone in the world of New
York, with an inordinate desire to shine before his
fellow-men, — his capital being a good face, a fair
knowledge of the classics, an illegible hand-writing,
and a fondness for society. Of dollars and cents
his supply became wofully scant. Accepting, accordingly, the first clerkship offered to him, he

filled it perfunctorily, but acceptably, though no prospect of his advancement was ever suggested; until his evil fortune lured him into falling in love with his employer's daughter, and inspired her cruelly to encourage him. She was rich, he over-scrupulous; her fortune was a barrier that he conceived to be insurmountable. The entanglement might thus have prolonged itself indefinitely, had not she, growing tired of it, forced him to show his hand and beg for hers. In answer she raised her eyebrows and wondered what he could mean. She was very sorry; she had never consciously given him cause to hope. How could he have misunderstood her so? Through an odd coincidence, but really nothing more, it happened, within a week, that her father resolved to reduce the sum-total of his salary-list by dispensing with Mr. Hazard's services. He was very sorry, — the family seemed conventional in its expression of regret, — but the business, etc., did not warrant, etc., etc., and Mr. Hazard could at any time rely, etc., etc., etc., upon his recommendation.

Poor Victor had been told, so often as to believe it, that a woman's " no " means " yes " at certain times. As in war the odds are all against the beleaguered city if the invaders stand their ground, so in love dogged persistence nearly always conquers in the end. In his heart of hearts he felt that he need only wait defiantly to gain this girl's admiration, pity, love. But once more his honest scruples overcame him. She was fabulously rich, he a beg-gar. In a weak moment he had miserably ignored this ; she had been to blame for the weakness which now led him to despise himself. He must prove to her, if possible, that he was no vulgar soldier of fortune ; he must bear defeat with dig-nity ; he could not hunt her down. He abandoned the field at once, and did his best to hate her. Can a man ever accomplish that when he has really loved the ideal woman his fancy has created ? Victor, certainly, made bad work of it ; he could not, even to himself, reproach this paragon. He only had been to blame. She was too good for him, for earth ; she was divine. He must never see her any more. He must put the ocean between them, and make his whole life a struggle to forget his own faultless line of beauty, eternally graven upon his heart, an indelible sorrow.

A friend, who half suspected his secret, stepped in at this critical moment and offered him an in-significant place on the staff of a great London banking-house. The pay was a mere pittance, ab-surdly small for his native city; he could barely live upon it even in London. But Victor accepted the terms gratefully, laughed hunger in the face, and told his anxious friend it should be made a stepping-stone to higher things. So he fled to the great heart of civilization as to a hermitage in the desert, lost his identity, and became a toiling unit in the ant-hill, a mere mechanic of routine. He carried letters of introduction which it pleased him to destroy unpresented. He made few acquaintances, fewer friends. Dick Purkitt was the only man who could be said to have grown intimate with him. And Purkitt did not know him long, before he felt that he should never know this odd stick of an American any better. Victor had been drawn to him, but not closely, never losing his head, never expanding. Dick remained baffled, but still interested; he took what Victor gave, and he asked no more, abused him for his false pride, and inwardly admired it.

Day after day Hazard bent over his desk in the huge, dingy counting-house, multiplying infinitely his journal-entries, till the load of dull monotony weighed upon him like the rock of Sisyphus. The room was favorably known in the City of London, and lay within a stone's throw of Threadneedle Street; it was low, ill-ventilated, and it quartered a small army of the overworked and underpaid beneath its glass ceiling, which admitted foggy light, in a qualified, commercial way, to fifty hollow-eyed and sallow faces. They could see, could be seen; what more was needed? By good or bad luck the American had found his allotted place near the only window in this dreary tread-mill. He could look up from his worn page, across a flagged court to the eastern wall of an old City church, whose chancel windows had at least imagination in them, — on the other side. Too often he caught himself trying to trace out their design, idly wondering about their colors. He never took the trouble to study them from the proper point within the church, — he never really cared a button for them. His day-dreams merely took this fragmentary shape in the beginning, piling up afterward like storm-clouds between him and the church-wall, till they had obscured it. Then his neighbor at the desk, alert, fond of work, and quick at figures, would jog his elbow, chaffing him.

"How many stones are there in that wall, Hazard? Are you going to build one like it?"

And the lynx-eyed bank-manager, noting Victor's lapse in duty, would make a mental black-mark against the truant understanding, and whisper to himself, —

"Hazard is a £100 clerk, — that's all."

Finally those dark stones did their destined mischief, and founded in Victor's heart the accursed fabric of a literary ambition. Why not, he thought, turn one's imagination to account, and help out one's bread-and-butter with *vin ordinaire*, if not with the intoxicating draught of fame? His first venture proved likewise his first misfortune, for he found an editor willing to accept it. All seemed plain sailing now. His boat was launched; he had but to let out the sheet and fly before the favoring breeze. But alas, the sky soon grew overcast, the sea troubled; the winds blew counter, or they died away. His ideas came to him slowly, painfully.

His little birds chirped, but did not sing; he set
them free to beat the air with feeble wings, to be
swept back and die unheard. The fumes of the
lamp got into his brain and clogged it. He tossed
through sleepless nights, while visionary clots of
blood, those danger-signals of the unresting train
of thought, swam before his staring eyes. Then
the long, stifling day at his desk became a terror
to him, the task a torture; he went to it with hag-
gard looks, as in a trance, performing it he knew
not how. But at night he lived again, still toiling
on in his garret under the stars. His own might
never rise, — well, so much the worse; he must
do without it. He had been bitten by the taran-
tula; he was dancing mad, and conscious of the
mania, could only murmur to himself, in bitter
consolation, the sad foreboding of the German
poet : —

> "One taste of the immortal fruit of fame,
> Like to Proserpina's pomegranate-seeds,
> Ranks thee forever with the quiet shades,
> And to the living thou belong'st no more." [1]

Now and then the tide up-bore him. When he
went to press, no matter how obscurely, all his courage would revive, and sanguine to absurdity, he
would expect too much; instant recognition from
the entire English-reading world; the meed of
genius; a horn of plenty overflowing at his feet, —
in short, miracles. And when all these failed

---

[1] Grillparzer's *Sappho ;* Ellen Frothingham's translation.

him, when the spheres coldly kept their course indifferent to his, he would sink down, down, each time a little lower, toward a despair of suicidal depth. His temper was fitful as the flight of an arrow shot over a sunlit glacier to miss its mark and fall into some crevasse beyond the glimpse of day.

The fit was on him that night; the fever first, and then the chill. When he begged Dick Purkitt for a hearing, he did so with the firm belief that the critic would warm at his work, would call it his best, perhaps the best that ever was. On the contrary the old hack had hardly pricked up his ears. He had been considerate, of course, — only damning with faint praise what had faintly touched him; that was enough. The fire was out in Victor's shabby lodging; at sight of the familiar room he shivered, but not with cold, — only with the remembrance of the half-frenzied hope he had carried away from the place earlier in the evening. His first impulse was to burn the ineffective masterpiece in the sputtering candle-flame. But he thought better of it; and mailed the manuscript to one of his editors, early the next morning, thus following Dick's advice, in part. For he did not begin upon another, did not even grope for a new idea; but only stared at nothing in a state of mental torpor, like a criminal awaiting sentence.

At least a fortnight must go by without an an-

swer; and the end of the year, always an anxious
time with Victor, was close at hand. He needed
money; he was not in debt, but on New Year's
Day there would be accounts to settle. He had
been a long time in the bank, had never missed
an hour, never asked for an increase of pay. It
occurred to him now to submit his case with becoming modesty, mildly to request what he felt
should be granted ungrudgingly at the first suggestion. If he was worth anything, he told himself, he was worth more than a paltry £100. Yet
he postponed the purposed interview, nervously
appointing ·to-morrow for it, and then to-morrow,
until at length Christmas and Boxing-Day came
next. Little time remained to lose ; it would be
better to decide the question before the holiday.
He watched his opportunity, and at last caught the
manager at leisure and alone. He was no advo-
cate; his voice faltered in the middle of a dis-
jointed phrase; the stern features of the judge
gave him no encouragement; the answer was short
and to the point.

"There are many young men in London, Mr.
Hazard, who would be glad to do your work for
£100."

Mr. Hazard admitted that, but —

"We cannot consider it; I am sorry, but the
fault is your own. They tell me you are trying to
serve two masters ; you will never get on so in
London. Do one thing or the other, and put your

heart into it. That is the best answer I can give you. Good-morning!"

The atom dropped back silently to its place in the swarm. In that short absence a black fog, dense, impenetrable, like a funeral veil, had settled down outside the window. Shreds of it even drifted in-doors and set the weaker ones to coughing, — they laughed and coughed again vaporously. The gas was lighted and soon burned out. Even London resources fail with sudden pressure put upon them. Candles glimmered about, and in the dim, smoky atmosphere the working-day went on. Nothing short of a convulsion of Nature can snap the main-spring of mercantile routine. Victor's senses were benumbed, and the hours seemed short to him; he forgot to give his usual sigh of relief when the clock struck and the night-birds were set free. The fog had grown thicker, heavier. He made his lonely way through it, from lamp to lamp, over the viaduct, along Holborn, in and out of the intricate Drury Lane quarter, to a stuffy coffee-house in Covent Garden, where, if the dinner was frugal, the beer was of the best. The foaming tankard quickened him; he could think now. But there was too much Christmas jollity in the place for him. He went out, took the shortest cut to the Strand, and reaching it, hesitated at the street corner. The sight was curious. Link-boys ran before the horses, shouting and brandishing their torches; a hurrying glare, with the barbaric light

of the past in it, that flashed by and left a deeper
gloom. It might have been a scene of Shake-
speare's time. The shops were crowded. In the
one behind him sprigs of holly and mistletoe
gleamed red and white through the frosted panes.
After a moment's thought Victor turned his face
toward Westminster. The way home was longer,
but that bridge cost nothing. When he came to
Charing Cross, the fog had lifted a little; he went
on, and it grew lighter; now he could see the shining clock-face in the Albert Tower; as he passed
under it the four quarters chimed out musically,
and the great bell struck the hour, — ten o'clock.
So late? Well, to-morrow was a holiday. The
lights glanced in the river, the steamers whistled,
the omnibuses rattled along the bridge. Overhead
a star sparkled, but he did not see it. He was
thinking of to-morrow.

"Do one thing or the other, and put your heart
into it."

Why? For what unprofitable purpose? Why
not let the tired muscles relax, the worn brain-
cells cease their reproduction?

Straightway he recalled some lines of his own
from a published story that had escaped critical
notice, so far as he knew; and he made them the
burden of his walk in mournful reiteration, —

"Man, in the struggle of life, is like a poor bull
baited in the arena, pricked and goaded and tor-
tured he knows not why, finding no escape;

before, behind him, only a great darkness closing in."

"That is true!" he cried as he turned the key in his lock. "Yes, that is true."

On the table lay a roll of paper, which he tore apart. His manuscript was returned with a printed word of formal thanks, — rejected. It was no less than should have been foreseen, but it struck Victor with the pang of a bullet.

"He might have written," he said; then dropped where he stood in tears.

After a time his face cleared itself and came out white and calm, firmly set with a new resolve. He tossed the manuscript with a dozen others into the grate and made a bonfire, crouching before it and warming his hands at the blaze. He blew out his lamp and paced the room awhile in the dark. Then, with a strange lightness of manner, he went back to the streets, leaving his door flung open wide behind him. The fog was almost gone, the air clearer and colder.

"To-morrow will be fine," he thought, following briskly a familiar course toward the City, — not that by which he had come, but the other, the shorter one, to Waterloo.

He smiled pleasantly at the toll-gatherer as he paid his fee. On the bridge he met only one man, — a muffled figure, breathing through a black band drawn tight over the lower part of the face, by way of precaution, not unusual, against the penetrating dampness of the English winter. The steps died away behind him ; he stopped at the middle of the bridge, and turned into a niche over one of its great piers. The light in his face had gone out ; he was cold now and trembling ; he leaned against the dank wall to steady himself. At that moment the mellow chimes of midnight, ushering in the Christian festival, pealed and echoed in a hundred spires ; the air seemed filled with music, — his ears hardly heard that sweetest of all sounds. He swung himself forward upon the wall.

" . . . only a great darkness closing in."

Nearer, — nearer. Now !

He had spoken no word. It was his action only that a voice behind him interrupted.

" Not yet ! " said the voice. A strong hand grasped him by the shoulder and pulled him back.

" Let me go ! " he cried imploringly ; and turning, found himself face to face with the stranger who had just passed him on the bridge. The figure unmuffled itself, removed the dark bandage from its mouth and chin, and stood before him revealed, recognizable.

" Mr. Rose ! " he gasped.

" You know my name, then. I see ; Purkitt told you. Yes, it is I, — Merlin Rose."

" Merlin Rose," repeated Victor, as though the name were a spell to conjure with. There was a kind of enchantment in this mysterious presence close upon him at this place and time.

"Mr. Hazard, is it not?"

"Yes."

"You wonder why I turned about. It was because I know your work and like it, — your brain-work, I mean. It may be that I can help you; if not, no harm is done."

"You know my work?" said Victor, startled and dazed by the unexpected word of praise.

"Yes; I once read a passage about life, that I have always remembered."

Thereupon he quoted the gloomy lines driven back that night like spectres to haunt the brain that had conceived them.

"Well, it is the truth," sighed Victor, in reply.

"An imperfect truth. You have stared at the sun through smoked glass. For better or worse, it was your only source of daylight. You need not have stared at it at all."

Victor's eyes filled, but he did not answer. The truth expressed itself in these lines also.

"Come!" said the other, in a kindly voice. "I have admired your courage, — let me do so still. You may be sure of my sympathy. Walk on with me out of the night-air, which I find dangerous. We will talk of your work, — it interests me."

Then Victor broke down completely. And his new friend soothed him with a quiet word or two and with gentle touches of the hand, as he would have comforted a tired child. They turned from that awful brink of suicide into the living tide of London, — ebb-tide now. Even the Strand was almost deserted ; the theatre-doors were shut, the jewelled eyes of their transparencies put out. But the loitering cab-man still hailed them from his perch ; the wine-shops kept open house, suffused with warm light, murmurous with voices.

As they walked and talked Victor drew closer to his companion, deeply interested, yet looking askance at him with a mixture of awe and fascination, partly due, no doubt, to Purkitt's tale. He had never seen so singular a face. It was gaunt, yet handsome ; the complexion a deep olive, very clear ; the heavy wrinkles in it came and went, sometimes vanished altogether. The eyes were still mere suggestions, remote, immovable points of blackness under the bushy, restless eyebrows. Something invisible cast over the man a perpetual shadow ; but through it he spoke emphatically, hopefully, — his praise took the form of a promise. Heights could be attained, rewards reaped, depending only upon courage. There was a way, a sure one, — the royal road it might be called, — if one dared try it. Then he hinted at a certain process to be undergone. Many had ventured to test its efficacy, always with a favorable result. But — and here he turned upon Victor that blank, scrutinous look, sharper in its effect than the chill of the winter's night — it wanted courage.

What of that promise ? Was there really some infusion or decoction to transmute mediocrity into genius ? — a subtle elixir, not of long life, but of inspiration ? Victor put a question, apparently foreign to the matter, but nevertheless a leading one.

"Are you a doctor by profession ?" he asked.

"No ; an engraver," replied the friend whom he half liked, half dreaded.

An engraver ! What a puzzling answer ! An odd chap this, as Dick had called him.

"Ah ! an inventor too, I suppose," continued Victor, quoting a part of Dick Purkitt's jocose description.

"Yes ; who has never invented anything," returned Mr. Rose, completing the jest with surprising fidelity. "Here we are ; wait a moment until I can strike a light. The stairs are steep."

He had stopped before a house in a narrow street curving out of St. Martin's Lane toward Leicester Square. On the ground-floor Victor noticed the closed shutters of a shop. One short flight, partitioned off from it, led them to the apartment overhead, where Mr. Rose inhabited three or four small rooms, low-studded and plainly furnished. One of these seemed to be his workshop, for it contained a drawing-board littered with engraver's tools ; passing this disorder by, he unlocked a small door and ushered his guest into a circular alcove, fitted up with some degree of

9

luxury, — a windowless place, heavily draped with curtains of dusky red that fell together over the door-way. Upon the low, concave ceiling a map of the world was painted. A fire burned brightly; two easy-chairs were drawn before it, and light streamed down upon them from an illuminated clock, the only ornament of the chimney-piece; on its glass dial seven clear-cut stars were scattered irregularly; through them the light shone more brilliantly, but with a soft, celestial radiance, white and still.

Over the clock hung a drawing in red chalk, — a young man's portrait, suggesting rather than resembling the first Napoleon.

"My own," said Mr. Rose, following the thought in Victor's eyes. "A good likeness, once."

And Victor, looking closely, saw that the sketch was signed, " Gérard."

On a round table in the middle of the room lay a thick folio bound in leather, with metal clasps which Mr. Rose drew back. Then he lifted one of the heavy covers and let it fall again.

"If I understand you rightly," he said, "you want certain things which I can give you, perhaps, should you trust me fearlessly."

"If you mean the world's notice and encouragement, — yes," Victor replied.

"In one word, — success," continued Mr. Rose. "But are you ready to pay the price? Not to me in money, — our vows prohibit that. We do not sell; we give. I refer to your own act of sacrifice, that calls for superhuman courage."

" What do you mean ? "

" This. Will you buy fame with mortal breath ? Will you run your allotted course, with all its trials, its possible triumphs, its unquestionable reverses ? Or will you snatch the Promethean fire, write your name in flaming letters, and die when this is done, shortening your life, it may be, by fifty of its years ? "

" More ! " cried Victor ; " by all but one ! Give me one glorious year to leave its mark behind it, and take the rest ! Death comes but once. Let mine come so."

" Ah ! " sighed Mr. Rose, " how many of you have made me the same answer ! Reflect, before it is too late. Even for immortality the cost is fearful."

" I have reflected," Victor returned. " In my dreams I have often made this very choice. If you can really offer it, my courage will not fail me. I am ready ; place me where I can choose."

In answer Mr. Rose opened the book before him.

" That you may see I am in earnest," said he, " read a few of the names that are written here. All these have in turn submitted themselves to me. Their lasting renown is your best security. I am to be trusted. See ! Not one that, living, was not famous ; that, dying, did not take his place among the stars. Read ! Read ! "

All the earlier pages of the volume were sealed together; but where it had opened, the loose leaves were inscribed with many signatures of the noble dead. Victor turned them slowly, coming at last to the name of a man still alive, already a celebrity. He started at the sight of it, recognizing at once the hand of his master, — Yarrow. All beyond was blank.

"I make but one condition," said Mr. Rose, as he put the pen into Victor's hand; "and that is absolute secrecy. You will never speak of this visit, or of me. Under the world's eye we do not know each other; remember that. You give me your word?"

"Yes," said Victor, signing without a moment's hesitation. "What more is there to do?"

"Your part is done," replied the other, in a low voice. "Sit here by the fire — a little nearer — so. Look up at the clock. I shall not detain you long."

His words died away in whispers. The minute-hand stood still. The flame behind it was steady, colorless; the stars were cold, like planets. Had they, like the planets, burned for ages? Could this unknown benefactor be in truth a Rosicrucian? No matter. His command must be obeyed blindly, blindly.

Victor bowed his head. Dusky spaces opened out before him. The power to move seemed lost; he could only stare down the black, endless dis-

tances, and listen to a faint sound, like the drum
of a bird far off in a forest. It is a dream, he
thought. A sharp pain shook him. No, it is
death, the after-thought came quivering. Then
he was there again, before the clock; a star was
gone. He counted them once more, — yes, there
were only six upon its face; but scarcely one
half-minute had passed over his head, and in the
chair beside him sat Mr. Rose, smiling, with a
small flask in his hand.

"I have done my part," he said. "The process
is performed, and here I give you the result. Use
it wisely."

Victor examined the flask. It contained a clear
liquid, faintly tinged with rose-color.

"What is this?" he asked.

Mr. Rose smiled again.

"You may call it, if you please," said he, "the
Tincture of Success."

"I see," said Victor, smiling back at him; "the
Frenchman's absinthe, or your English opium, —
a draught of inspiration. Your health! I drink
to you."

Mr. Rose caught his hand.

"Not one drop of it!" he cried. "Go
home, and mix that with your ink. To-morrow,
take your pen and write, without undue excitement, slowly, thoughtfully, laboriously, as most
men do."

"Is that all?" Victor asked with an air of

disappointment. The royal road, then, was the turnpike still.

"No, when the ink is gone, bring the flask to be filled again. Come at this same hour, between night and morning. Remember, silence. No word of this to any one. Good-night! Dismiss all fear of discouragement; that time is past. For you, the struggle of life is over."

Victor shivered. These parting words conveyed a double meaning. But he had made his choice, had signed the compact; it was irrevocable. That fear too must be dismissed, if possible.

Weeks went by, quietly enough; but before long, he felt that an unaccountable change had come over him. By day he worked at the bank with a feverish lightness, like that preceding his arrested act of suicide. At night his ink flowed more freely than of old. His thoughts came thick and fast; it was hard to hold them back, to write cautiously, in obedience to Mr. Rose's warning. His first manuscript, sent out with something of his former distrust and hesitancy, was at once accepted, afterward, in print, warmly praised. Others soon followed it; perceptibly he gained in reputation. At the end of six months when his flask had been filled for the third time, he was called the rising young author. Then, turning his back upon his irksome employment in the City, he trusted wholly to his pen, and to the mysterious influence that guided it; pro-

duced his first important work; was known to
fame.

The subtle process, to which he owed so much,
varied only in degree. Always the same chair
awaited him; always he whirled away into the
same outer darkness. But each time, while the
gloom grew vaster and more oppressive, the distant drumming sound came nearer, and was followed by a sharper pain, a certainty of death
more imminent and more appalling. Always,
when he woke, another star had disappeared from
the clock-face. Yet always no appreciable moment had been wasted. There sat his generous
host, smiling inscrutably, watching him with eyes
he could not see, bestowing the priceless gift,
then curtly dismissing him, reluctant even to
accept his thanks. Once only Victor ventured
to prolong his visit, to describe his sensations, to
beg for some word of explanation; but Mr. Rose
shook his head mournfully, laid his finger upon
his lips, and Victor knew that he was never to
know more.

Dick Purkitt had been the first to congratulate
him. At the second stage of progress the good
fellow threw up his hat and cheered.

"I always knew you had it in you, dear boy.
Damn it, did n't I tell you so? Your name is
Victor. Keep it up; keep it up!"

And then when Victor left the garret and the
bank, moving northward and westward into com-

fortable lodgings, Dick called upon him, and em-
braced him with tears of joy in his eyes. Suddenly he stopped, holding the rising author off
at arm's length, inspecting him in his critical
way.

"I say, young-un, what's the matter? You
look poorly. Are you overworked? What is it,
man?"

"Nothing," said Victor.

But Dick shook his head uneasily. Did he
sleep? Did he eat? Did he take his consti-
tutional? Something must be devilish wrong.
What was it?

"Nothing," Victor insisted.

Nothing; yes, nothing he could explain. But
there was something devilish wrong, indeed, — a
haunting terror, constant, merciless, indefinable,
of which he could not speak. For him the future
had become the present; the sun no longer shone.
His horizon-line was lost, and he walked in twilight on the verge of a gulf beset with shadows.
The nameless dread consumed him like a wasting
disease. He hardly knew his own eyes in the
glass; they had a restless, hunted look, forever
turning backward over the shoulder which Mr.
Rose had grasped, as if they feared an encounter
with the supernatural. His one relief was in his
work; discovering that, he gave himself up to
it with untiring devotion. Success followed hard
upon success; rich rewards lay heaped around

him ; even the voice of petty jealousy was hushed ; and as the note of triumph swelled louder and deeper, into one long, harmonious acclaim, he resigned love, liberty, everything for that, accepting the substitute eagerly, gratefully, with a fierce, inhuman joy. For this he had given the death-blow to his own happiness ; but he knew no remorse and no repentance ; he was borne on in speechless agony, unflinching.

One day there came a letter that stirred him. It was from a man he had never known, once his chosen master, — Yarrow. The veteran conqueror had turned hermit, producing little of late, fencing himself off from the world. So it happened that Victor and he had never met. The message was an expression of his delight in the fine quality of the younger man's work, a wish that they might know each other. He was ill, and, therefore, could not call upon Mr. Hazard. Would not Mr. Hazard waive ceremony, and come to him ? Victor did so immediately. He had long desired such an interview ; it was now brought about in the best possible way, giving promise of pleasure to them both. Instead of that it proved on both sides extremely painful. Victor was shown through a splendid house into a darkened chamber, where the sick man sat, propped up with pillows, tossing and turning restlessly. As he came forward Yarrow's look of welcome changed to one of deep compassion.

"You, too —" he murmured, then checked himself, and offered his hand in silence.

And Victor at first could say nothing. Death was written in the face; he knew the lines by heart, — he had learned them in his own. They talked awhile in broken whispers, each struggling for self-control. It was useless; the open secret was there; they could neither mention nor ignore it. So they parted as they had met, silently, with blurred eyes and trembling lips, their sympathy expressed only in a lingering, convulsive clasp of hands.

A few hours later Victor Hazard paid his seventh and, as it proved, his last visit to Mr. Rose. The signs for the moment were all the same. He lay in the dark, bound hand and foot; the noise began, the deadly pain followed; but now, for the first time, the sound defined itself: clearly, it could only be the sharp, continuous rattle of hammers plied by dexterous hands. He woke with a start to find himself alone, holding the flask once more refilled. But the clock burned dimly; not a single star was left in it; and the noise, for once, did not cease. He had brought it back with him; it was there in the house, echoing around him, above, below, at his very feet. He called his host by name. No one answered; he was, indeed, left quite alone. He found the door and went out into the work-shop. There stood the drawing-board with the tools lying upon it; another object too that caught his eyes, attracting him, — a shining strip of silver, upon which had been engraved two dates, a name. He started, turned faint, and clutched the table. The name was Yarrow.

He waited there for some time in a kind of stupor, fearing to move, lest at a step he should fall insensible. Meanwhile, the noise went on. He could not endure it; he must get out into the air. The street was very near, the staircase short; he knew his way perfectly. With a painful effort, he dragged himself slowly down, supported, as he went, by the partition-wall. Ah! The noise grew louder, coming from the shop of course. What were they doing there? He had never seen the place; it had been black and silent always. What journeymen were busy in it now, at such an hour, hammering, hammering, as though they would wake the dead? Here was the street-door; the handle turned, the fresh air revived him. Through the barred shutters at his side there peeped a ray of light. Where light was, he could see. He gave one look, only one. The shop was an undertaker's. The men were driving nails into a coffin.

He recoiled, shuddering. Something hurt his hand. It was only his precious flask, clinched a shade too tightly. He flung it from him now with all his might. He heard the glass strike the opposite wall and shiver into fragments. Then he staggered away, muttering incoherently, losing himself in the night-fog, wandering over London; but somehow bringing himself out at his own door, beating at it, to be found there by the servants, a stained and draggled heap upon the threshold; to be told long afterward, that at this very moment the mighty presses of Fleet Street, — as they rose and fell in harsh, metallic rhythm, to note the price of corn, the last division of the House, all affairs of all men, great and small alike, — were stamping out with iron feet the life and death of Yarrow.

That morning Victor Hazard woke delirious, in a raging fever. He rallied, sunk, became gradually weaker, and never left his room again. Doctors consulted over his case, called it hard names, and shook their heads, impotent as Belshazzar's sooth-sayers. Through it all his old friend, Dick Purkitt, was constant at his bedside. And now at last Victor returned Dick's friendship, confided in him, even to that unfinished romance of early life, — the broken round of a ladder leading to the clouds. But one secret he still kept back, — he never spoke of Mr. Rose; never so much as hinted at the Tincture of Success.

One day Dick found him lying there with a sealed package in his hand, looking at it doubtfully, turning it about with thin, nervous fingers.

" What is that ? " Dick asked.

Victor held it up, showing the address of a certain Miss Ashburnham in New York. Underneath he had written, " After my death to be delivered."

" Ah ! " said Dick, " now I understand."

" Understand ?   What ? "

Then he was told that often in his delirium he had worried about some letters, undoubtedly these, that were sometimes to be burned, sometimes sent off by the next post.

" Yes," said Victor, " her letters.   I have always kept them so.   Burn the package, Dick.   I added a line of my own, long ago; to receive it now might give her pain."

" Let her have it," Dick replied.   " She deserves to suffer, but she won't.   You can't hurt her as she hurt you.   Send it along."

" No ; we will burn them."

And they were burned, unopened.

It had now become apparent that Victor could not live through the week.   Three days later he showed Dick another letter, just received, from Miss Ashburnham.

It was a long letter, and its real significance lay all between the lines.   She had followed his work, had always admired it.   She knew he was ill, but not seriously, she hoped and believed.   He must surely be destined to a long and happy life.   Then, referring to the past, she confessed that she had been much to blame.   Would he not forget the wrong she had done him ?   Would he not send her a line to say she was forgiven ?

Without a written word of love, the letter invited a declaration in every syllable. " She thinks it worth while, now, blast her ! " Dick remarked to himself. Like most bachelors of forty-five he had his own private views of woman's gentle nature ; but he waited to see what would come of it, exerting no undue influence. Victor called for a pen that only scrawled illegibly and slipped from his hand.

" Let me write," said Dick.

Victor shook his head.

" No ; I will not answer it. I have outgrown all that. Even if I lived, I could never love her, — never any woman. Burn it, Dick, as we burned the others."

He looked idly at the flame, while Purkitt stirred it with fiendish satisfaction ; then he dozed away. Dick sat by and watched him. An hour after he woke.

" Dick," he asked in a hoarse, labored whisper, " how long have I been at it ? "

" What do you mean, Victor ? At what ? "

" Success," he answered feebly, — " success, I mean."

" Not quite three years, old man."

" All that ? Nearer, Dick, nearer; I can't speak up. Tell me, is it real, — will it last, — will my work live ? "

" Surely, dear boy, surely. It is great. On my soul, I believe so," said Dick, struggling to keep down the tears.

A smile stole over Victor's face, and he slept awhile longer peacefully. Then he woke for the last time, starting up in bed, wandering.

"Dick!" he cried, tugging at his shirt, as though something stifled him. "Dick! I put my heart into it. See!"

He fell back, with the shirt torn open, revealing seven star-shaped scars upon his breast, above the heart already stilled. Dick saw and wondered at them. He never knew that they were the seven stars of Man's Destiny, the mystic symbols of the Rosicrucian brotherhood, and that through them, drop by drop, the first ingredient in the Tincture of Success had been drained away.

THE ROCK OF BÉRANGER.

I WAS still a young man ('t is twenty years since then) when I first made the journey into Switzerland. And I paraded a fine festival-flower of enthusiasm, which ought to have been immensely gratifying to the jaded senses of older travellers, but which my one companion did his very best to blight, — with no success whatever. We were thrown into the close intimacy of travel for little more than a fortnight, and we never have journeyed together again. But this is due rather to the sundering force of outward circumstances than to our peculiar dissimilarity of sentiment, remarkable as that undeniably was. When we meet at rare intervals, we still smile over some half-forgotten incident of that memorable comradeship, — we have so little else in common to smile over. For he is gruff and grizzled; his oldest child is in society, and of all but her he is now more ruthlessly critical than ever. He has his wife to ko-tow before him, ugly old Chinese curio that he is! while I —

It was at a crowded *table d'hôte* in Geneva that fate, one August night, allotted me a chair next to

Hans Worden, whom I took for a German at first, —
not on account of his name, which I did not know.
He has, in fact, a drop or two of Dutch blood in
his veins, but is as thorough-paced an American as
any ever shod, and this I soon discovered. I saw
too that he was broad-shouldered and bald, with a
spike of hair upon his forehead; that he wore a
stiff yellow beard and moustache, clipped into
bristles; that he must be at least ten years my
senior, and must measure considerably less than
two yards in height, but almost all of that in the
girth. His answers were short and somewhat too
direct. Though we were alone in a crowd, and I
was lonely, I did not care for him. But when I,
by an awkward accident, projected half my pint of
vieux Macon into his portion of the *raie au beurre
noir*, he was unexpectedly civil about this trying
circumstance, which he certainly could not have
foreseen. On that account I felt bound to him by
a tie of gratitude, and accordingly tried to say as
little as I could, and to say it in his way. This
flattered him, perhaps, for he began to do his share
of the talking, and when dinner was over he invited me to take coffee and *fine champagne* with
him upon the terrace. There, continuing our talk,
we found that we had friends in common at home,
that we were still alone in the crowd, that we were
going the same way on the morrow. The twilight
grew murky round our ears, the lighthouse flashed
out upon the jetty; the lake lapped the shore

10

gently; under the wall a wandering Savoyard
struck up a plaintive love-song; and in the dark
we exchanged the cigar of peace and became fellow-
travellers.

The next day, which seemed interminable, we
took the steamer for Chillon. I was oppressively
conscious of myself, all the time on guard against
the possibility of boring my new acquaintance; to
do that would not be difficult, I felt. He did not
bore me, but he hampered me by his indifference
to the cool northwesterly breeze, the sunshine, the
glistening water. I could not get accustomed to
his presence; he was constantly on my mind, and
yet I was lonelier than I should have been without
him. I did not demand exciting incidents; I found
room for diversion in the mere sight of these new
shores. But here, at my back, hung my Old Man
of this inland Sea, who would neither divert himself nor let me be diverted.

At Chillon I let myself go, and enjoyed things in
my own way, which was not at all like his; but
he was not bored, and seeing this I took heart and
found his attitude amusing. The oubliettes and
cells of the condemned he inspected gravely, but
with a shrug of the shoulders. A certain torture-
post, that bore marks of heated iron, looked, he
said, as if it had been freshly roasted over night
for our especial benefit; and this I could not deny.
Concerning Bonnivard he was reticent and scepti-
cal, but two or three of the famous names carved

in the dungeon pillar he read aloud with a faint show of interest. Just above Lord Byron's, one of our own nation, a female sculptor, or, as she would say, a sculptress, had recorded herself in letters an inch long. The name, newly cut, had not hardened in the limestone, and with the stick he carried Worden quietly obliterated it. One swift stroke of the ferule, and it was gone. Here, for the first time, we were in perfect sympathy. From that moment I knew we should get on.

And so we did admirably. Worden took the lead and made the pace, while I followed, frequently out of step, but always within hailing distance. That night we passed in Vevey at the famous hostelry of the Three Crowns, well termed grandiose by the fluent author of the guide-book. This straightforward work, by the way, was Worden's pet aversion, — the scarlet of its covers made his eyes flash fire like a bull's; in vain I protested that much wisdom lay between them, and that we were ignorant. I might keep it by me, he said, might even quote from it, if I chose, — he could not prevent that; but it must never be flaunted about in his presence. We were not tourists, " doing " things from a mistaken sense of duty; we were moving this way and the other way, as our souls incited us, for pleasure only; God willing, without formulæ.

For our pleasure, therefore, we descended at the Three Crowns; walked out toward a glowing sunset, and turning, saw its colors die away in the

distant peak of the Dent du Midi; while just across
the lake, from behind the crags of Meillerie, a
storm-cloud raised its head, glaring and growling
fitfully like some monstrous chimera of the mountains. Then the unexpected happened, and we
encountered a wonderful Russian princess of literary tendencies, who greeted Worden heartily.
"What! Not married yet?" she inquired. And
upon his answer in the negative, we were given the
freedom of her salon, a marvel of barbaric luxury,
overhanging the lake, where we took coffee and
liqueurs, and smoked, all three; while she told tales
of obvious point in many languages, and deplored
our early departure.

"I came here for a month," she said, "and lo, I
have stayed three years. There is no place like it
in all Europe. But to-morrow you will leave me."
And when we assured her that our one desire was
to be always there with her, but that — she sighed,
and said all men were of the brutes and cruel.
One might have done worse than to accept her
lotus-branch thus invitingly extended; but as Worden remarked afterward, one usually does worse,
somehow, on this side of the planet.

"What! Not married yet?" The woman of
the world had asked it with a note of intention
that kept recurring to me. Did he want to marry,
then? Was that the clew to his incapacity for
enjoyment, his pre-occupation, his feverish desire
to push on — for pleasure — to see all, and think

of nothing? Pleasure, indeed! Could he see anything as I saw it? Could he dismiss from his mind the thought I did not know? Was he not really blind with some old pain, and brooding always upon that? The fancy stole into my brain and would not out of it. *Habet!* The princess knew what she was talking about. A woman has jilted him; he is trying to forget her.

His face and figure had a wofully comic cast in them. He was not the man to command affection at a moment's notice; not at all the kind of lover that I, for instance, would make if my time ever came. But in spite of that, perhaps because of it, my interest in him deepened wonderfully. The quenchless spirit of opposition, that I laughed at, became charged with pathos now. I understood his imperfect sympathy with the landscape, his contempt for the beautiful, even among women, — all of whom he affected to regard as of a race apart, inferior to our own. Evidently this was a case of acute mental strabismus, — his mind's eye, turning inward and not outward, caught but a poor half-light, distorting everything.

Constant and severe as his pangs must have been, they were not permitted to impair his appetite. We put up, accordingly, for our next mid-day meal at the queer old town of Saint Maurice, in the Rhone valley, where, after our first word or two, the smiling peasant-maiden of the inn treated us with great deference, yet with unaccountable famil-

iarity.   Never was a simple second breakfast served
with such circumstance, with such chattering about
each dish as it was set down.

"For whom does she take us?" I asked. "I
told her in my best accents that we were voyaging
to Chamouni from the Three Crowns."

"For princes of the blood, perhaps," said Worden. "Eat your gruyère with a good conscience.
If need be, I will assume the rôle."

He had hardly spoken when to us entered the
landlord, carrying a bottle of choice wine, which he
pressed upon our acceptance. Without knowing
why, we were forced to drink his health, and with
much bowing and scraping he pledged us, in return,
enduring prosperity.

"And since it appears," he added, "that these
gentlemen travel onward in the service of the
Three Crowns — " Thereupon, drawing from his
pocket a handful of the hotel cards, he begged the
gentlemen to honor him by distributing these in
his favor along their road.

My lips parted for a shout of derision, but Worden silenced me with a look. Quietly accepting the
situation and the cards likewise, he told our host
that we would do all in our power to oblige him.
The sharp-eyed Switzer fairly beamed; he had
known intuitively that we were men of much dis-
tinction; but when informed by his servant that
the first and second butler of the famous Three
Crowns chose to sustain themselves awhile with

him in a course of recreation, he had felt that his
best would be all too poor and crude for palates of
such refinement; and he prayed our indulgence,
since he was thus taken unawares. Of course the
stupid girl had either misinterpreted my statement
or had wilfully embellished it. And here stood
Worden nodding assent to all this with the utmost
tranquillity. I could not control my features, and
left the room abruptly for space to laugh in.

Upon the rough pavement before the door lay
stretched a huge dog of Saint Bernard, snapping at
the flies, and round the corner of the house I saw
our coachman and another of his class consorting
with the foolish, tittering maid; otherwise the street
was vacant. Absurdly narrow and primitive, it
was, nevertheless, the main thoroughfare of the
town. Halfway down the opposite side a rival
hotel displayed its sign of blue and gold. "We
should have gone there," I thought; "it is the
better house of the two." The guide-book, to which
I now tardily referred, confirmed me in this impression. Just then the little group of Swiss broke
up, the strange man lounging off to the stable-yard
of the other establishment, out of which he presently reappeared, this time on the box of a well-
appointed travelling-carriage that drew up at the
opposite door. Wraps were stored away in front,
trunks were strapped behind; a handsome old
fellow with gray hair took his place upon the back
seat; the bustle subsided, the street was still again;

but the old man waited on, impatiently glancing up
at one of the windows.

"Yes, Papa, I am coming," called down to him
in English a silvery voice. And in a moment
more the daughter came. The coachman shouted,
cracked his whip; the horses tossed their heads as
they dashed by me. All were gone in a flash along
the road we had just passed over, not the one we
were to follow. The merest glimpse was allowed
me of a pretty face half-veiled, a pair of brown eyes
bent on me coquettishly, as I could not help believ-
ing; but that glimpse I caught.

"Atrocious chance!" I muttered. "If we had
gone to the other house; if they had only turned
our way!"

Worden now appeared, with the jovial landlord
still in attendance to speed our departure by strong
injunctions to the driver for our safe-conduct and
by renewed expressions of good will toward us.

"Did you undeceive him?" I asked when we
also were well out of the town, but in the wrong
direction.

"No," said Worden. "Why spoil the joke, and
make the worthy man uncomfortable? He actually
declined, at first, to give me a bill for our breakfast. But I told him it was not our habit to demand such favors. Why did you take yourself
off?"

"For a pair of bright eyes, Monsieur the Butler-
in-chief," I answered. Looking back down the

valley as I spoke, I caught sight of the other carriage afar off, a mere speck upon the Villeneuve road. "And after the eyes I flung my heart; see, it is there."

Then I informed him in a word that we should have gone to the other hotel, and why. But he congratulated himself upon our fortunate escape.

"Some school-girl in vacation," he continued. "A bundle of American nerves, as your description proves, — given to sheep's-eyes and hysterics. Bah! Did you notice the young person who waited upon us just now at the inn? Admirably robust."

That afternoon he did amiably enough all that was expected of him, alighting for a nearer view of the lovely waterfall with an unspeakable name, and in the Gorge du Trient following up the wooden gallery to its very end. At both places he amused himself by sticking his hotel cards into every crevice of rock he could find.

"To whom it may concern," he explained. "Was I not asked to distribute them along the road?"

Then observing the look of satisfaction on the face of the coachman, who posed as our guide to all the wonders of the wayside, Worden added, —

"The end is not yet. We shall reap our reward for this, as you will see."

Oddly enough, we did so almost immediately. For upon arriving at Martigny we found the hotel crowded to overflowing. It appeared for a moment as if we must sleep under the stars. But the coachman whispered to the *portier*, the *portier* to the *chef de bureau;* and behold, we obtained a gem of a salon with two alcoves, upon the main floor fronting the prospect.

"We are powers in the land!" cried Worden, the deceiver. "I have mastered the art of European travel. I am a butler evermore."

"A false position may have its inconveniences," I suggested.

"Stuff and nonsense!" he retorted. "I tell you we are kings!"

That night our coachman, Victor, who knew the mountains, begged for the privilege of guiding us across them. We could ride the horses, he said; and for the luggage, there was the sweetest of joyous little mules, eager for employment, to be had for a song. Of course we closed with him at once.

"There, you see," said Worden; "we carry all before us, — even to the mules."

I could only hope meekly that good would come of it. So we got up with the sun, and went on, bag and baggage, horse and mule and foot, over the pass of the Tête-Noire, — a route "common-hackneyed in the eyes of men," as my companion took great pains to tell me. But what of that? I had not seen it, nor had he. Was ever cynic argument so weak? Must we give up the Rhine, then, because poets for ages have loved to call it blue, when it wears, in fact, the yellowish-green hues of jade? Has the photograph solved the riddle of the Sphinx;

and is she, from over-scrutiny, no more inscrutable ?
Shall we hunt for new sensations in the heart of
Ethiopia and the squalid suburbs of great cities ?
No, thank Heaven! The Old World's face is not
worn out so easily by vulgar eyes. The Tête-Noire
was my first mountain-pass, and it will always be my
best one. The view of the winding Rhone from the
height of the Forclaz still remains to me a marvel ;
and the dark wilderness of fir-trees along the sharp
descent to the hidden torrent of the Eau Noire
overshadows my remembrance, as though it were
the *selva oscura* of the " Inferno." Great sheets
of mist enveloped us there that day. The wind
howled, the rain beat down ; but, save only the
mule who was no longer joyous, we jogged on
merrily.

" Behold ! " cried Victor, pointing with his staff
to a boundary-stone by the roadside ; " La France ! "
And out of a chest of appalling depth he intoned
the Marseillaise. So with a song on our lips we
came down into Savoy ; and all around us, but invisible through the driving mist, lay the vale of
Chamouni.

Suddenly, high above me, on my left, the nearer
clouds parted for an instant and disclosed an
enormous mass of heaped-up crystals, pale-blue in
color, towering into space and ending there abruptly, like the broken arch of a rainbow. I could
not trust my eyes, and thought the light had
played some trick upon them.

" Look there ! " I called to Victor. " Do you see that ? "

"Does not Monsieur know ? " he answered calmly. " It is the glacier of Argentière."

The fog swept back, and it was gone. It had seemed as far removed from earth as the summer-cloud that melts before one's eyes never to re-assume its former shape, unreal as a vision. I was convinced that I should never find that light again in Argentière or any other glacier. And, indeed, none has ever looked to me as that did then.

Night overtook us ; the storm grew fiercer. We could hardly see our horses' heads ; we were soaked to the skin. But the village lights shone larger and brighter, and before long we plunged in among them, found our hotel, and steamed before a roaring fire. The old comedy of whispers went on between Victor and our last new landlord, who immediately transferred us to luxurious quarters befitting the state we had again tacitly assumed. Worden's eyes twinkled as he pulled from his pocket various cling-ing masses of wet pasteboard, reduced almost to their original pulp by the penetrating rain.

" May Saint Boniface, patron of hotels, grant me his forgiveness ! I quite forgot them."

" You did your duty by them yesterday, Heaven knows," said I.

" Not a bit of it," he returned. " These were given to me this morning. They are the hotel cards of Martigny."

" Then I, for one, will wear a wine-label no longer. I shall go down immediately and disclose the whole fraudulent business to the gentlemanly proprietor."

" And lose these rooms !" cried Worden, catching me by the arm. " Are you mad ? Leave everything to me. I 'll discuss all the vintages of the country with them, if necessary. Hold your tongue, and let the innocent fraud go on. It hurts nobody ; besides I like it."

He had his way. Nothing was said, and we remained marked men and honored.

The next sun came blazing up into a cloudless sky, rousing me at an early hour and drawing me out upon the balcony, while I was still clothed in picturesqueness. With the silent wonder of youth I beheld the narrow, level meadows and the brawling Arve, the great brown crags rising abruptly on either side through their green fringes to snow-fields of dazzling whiteness, leading up at last to one clear summit whiter than them all. I needed no guide to tell me which among these peaks was royal. There he sat with his guards around him, high on his immutable throne, splendid as a god. I had slept for hours at his feet in the darkness of ignorance. Now I knew all upon the instant, as if at the touch of an enchanter's wand.

I went along the balcony and startled Worden out of a sound sleep. Just as he was, I dragged him to the window.

"Well, what of it?" he said, rubbing his eyes.

"The Mont Blanc!" I stammered.

He yawned audibly. "Disappointing, is n't it? I have seen more snow than that in Madison Square."

"Good-by," I said, making for the balcony. "I give you up."

"Wait a bit. What time is it?"

"Seven o'clock."

"Why on earth did you wake me? I was having such a superior dream; I shall never know the end of it now. No matter; coffee with you in just two hours." And he went to bed again.

What could be done with such dull eyes as these? Nothing, I concluded, but religiously to let them alone. The scheme worked to perfection. Upon coming in that morning from my first solitary stroll, I found Worden pacing his room furiously. Where had I been? Why had I crawled off by myself? If there was anything to see, he wanted to see it. For what else had I brought him? I aped humility, proposing that we should take shares forthwith in one of the village guides, and explore the neighborhood exhaustively and systematically. There fell to our lot, as it happened, a friend of Victor, who on departing that day for his native pastures assured us that we should find the guide Franz a good comrade, very sure of foot; and so he proved. I caught a sharp attack of the climbing fever, which communicated itself in a milder form to Worden; though I could not help suspecting that his interest, such as it was, in our daily life arose less from my influence than from the contents of a certain telegraphic message that came to him, as it were, out of a clear sky. What information it gave I had no means of knowing, but I could see that it was of a soothing nature.

As it now appeared. that he desired to go where I went, he was dragged up the Flégère and down the Brévent; over the Mer de Glace, and under it to the crypt-like source of the Arveiron; through half the long list of *courses ordinaires*, — treating everything lightly, turning all he could into ridicule; and if nothing was left him but to admire, undemonstrative. When I asked why feelings were given him never to be expressed, he replied that since I expressed mine so well, competition would be useless; it seemed to him, sometimes, that I had feelings enough for two. And with this shaft of sarcasm I was for the time silenced, if not convinced.

It was pleasant to see him perched on the wiry apex of a mule, following my lead now, up many a zigzag bridle-path, along the verge of many a precipice; always imperturbable, even when the beast who bore him craned its neck toward some scrubby thistle-blossom a yard or two down the awful gulf. He consented, though reluctantly, to have his shoes spiked when I inclined to glaciers. But upon one point neither I nor Franz could shake his strong opinion. He pronounced the common mountain-staff, or alpenstock, tipped with goat-horn and smoothly rounded to the hand, a foolish and de-testable encumbrance,—chiefly, I think, because cus-tom makes it also an Alpine souvenir, by branding it with names and other data in a decorative spiral. Every village cobbler has his set of iron type ready for heating and stamping at a small fee. In Cha-mouni our windows commanded that functionary's little shop, and the line of tourists constantly closing in at his door to have their exploits indeli-bly recorded. This exhibition of innocent weakness always stirred Worden to wrath.

"A melancholy sight!" he said once. "The world depresses me hourly more and more. Look at that string of people, — every mother's son and daughter in it a fool, if not a liar! For, of course, all the feats in Switzerland, whether performed or not, are duly chronicled; and each stick that comes goes home with 'Aiguille Verte' burned into it, or I'm a Dutchman!"

"The Aiguille Verte is inaccessible," I ventured to remonstrate.

"But the letters of the alphabet are not, my boy. They may be bought for one centime apiece, as I am informed; and that wretched shoemaker will die a millionnaire through the folly of your coun-trymen."

"Let the ill wind blow him good," said I. "It does no harm to you."

" Yes ; it does. It strokes me the wrong way ; it
ruffles my sweet temper. See that sexless thing
with a veil around its head. Is it a man or
a woman? Neither; it's an American tourist,
personally conducted. Pah! Let us do the
Aiguille Verte to-morrow, if only to escape from
such monstrosities."

The morrow for that rash attempt never came,
though we prolonged our stay in Chamouni, — on
the whole, no worse a place than any other, Worden said ; but this admission, be it noted, was
made after the receipt of a second mysterious tele-
gram. We had been there ten days before I was left
alone again. All that morning rain had threatened;
the afternoon promised to be clear, and I therefore
suggested a climb along the Glacier des Bossons to
its attendant cascade. Worden said he was sleepy,
and would rather dream about it ; but I must go,
that he might know the place through my emotions
afterward. I consequently set out with Franz, on
foot, and took the walk so leisurely that when we
came back into the high-road, a mile below the
village, the sun was already out of sight. The
afternoon had climbed too, and had outstripped us ;
but to follow it we needed only to lift our eyes, for
overhead the peaks still shone, keeping night at
bay a little longer. There was not the smallest
hurry, and I stopped first to examine a rough wayside shrine with its glazed portrait of the Madonna,
then to drink from a spring that trickled over

some mossy rocks near by. Franz pulled out his pipe.

"It is not late," said I. "Let us sit here and smoke comfortably. Hark, I hear horses. Is that the diligence from Geneva?"

"No," said Franz, after cocking his head to listen. "That is not the diligence."

The click of the hoofs drew rapidly nearer. We watched curiously a turn of the road, round which in a few moments the travellers must reveal themselves. Suddenly the sound stopped. Then we heard voices raised in discussion. Apparently the strangers had come to grief, and were bewailing it in at least two languages. My ear detected the confusion of tongues, but not the words.

Franz caught up his ice-axe and coil of rope.

"An accident!" he cried dramatically. "To the rescue!" It proved to be no more than a broken trace. O Fortune! No more, and very much more. For here were the self-same father and daughter who had been whirled away from me out of Saint Maurice. He did not recognize me at first; in such a case the father never does. But the girl's cheeks colored a little when our eyes met. She knew instantly that they had met before, and she remembered where.

While Franz and the coachman mended the harness, the old man thanked me for our timely aid. He had seen my face, he thought, but could not tell when.

"Ten days ago," I explained; "in the Rhone valley."

"At Saint Maurice, Papa;" his daughter added.

"Oh, to be sure," said he, with a smile. "You must have come the other way."

"Yes," I answered, silently wondering why the fact should afford him any amusement. An awkward pause followed, during which I read the words painted on one of the trunks : HARGRAVE, NEW YORK. Their nationality would thus have been established, had any doubt of it existed in my mind. The man's features were of a good American type ; the fashion of his gray beard and a scar upon his forehead gave him a martial look. "A veteran of the last war!" I thought. "Colonel, perhaps, or General — General Hargrave!" The girl was very like him, with brown hair and eyes, and a very clear complexion; an imperious and fascinating little beauty of one or two seasons, — not a school-girl. She, of course, was Miss Hargrave, though it appeared that I was not to be told this formally. Well, introduction was a bore; I should make no move in its direction. I knew her name, what did mine matter?

"Jump in, Letty!" said the old soldier, "and tell the man to walk his horses. The village is very near, and I sha' n't run any risks. Won't you take the other seat?" he asked, turning to me.

I excused myself. I would go with them, but on foot.

Upon further talk, as we proceeded, I thought the acquaintance was, in a certain way, too informal. They were evidently trying to be civil, but the effort was always apparent, and at times my presence seemed to be ignored. It was too late for me to drop behind; I could only keep on with them, and do my best to seem at ease. Finding that they had never been in Chamouni, I pointed out its wonders, calling the mountain-tops by their names familiarly. Miss Hargrave listened and admired, but with some absence of mind. Suddenly she asked me if there were many Americans at the hotels.

Her father gave a dry cough, as if to emphasize her words or his own. "Do you expect to find anybody," he asked,—"anybody whom you know?"

She shook her head, and brought the talk directly back again to the view.

"It is finer than all the rest," she said, "but we are too far below it; I want to climb up, up, away from people,—American people, I mean."

This speech struck me as most discourteous under the circumstances, and for a moment I was confounded by it. Did she take me for some outlandish foreigner? Or, worse than that, was I a nobody, to be forgotten, as well as ignored? Her words had made her father smile unconsciously.

"Why do you always laugh, Papa?" she asked.

"I was n't laughing," he replied, becoming preternaturally solemn at once. But I saw the smile

getting the better of him the moment her attention
was diverted.

"Are the hotels good?" she inquired of me.

I was not forgotten then. Her rudeness was
unintentional of course; to her I was a foreigner.
How could I have doubted it? The joke was capital; but what kind of foreigner, I wondered.

"Oh, yes," I returned, "as hotels go. They are
not grandiose, — not like the Three Crowns."

"Naturally not," she said with what seemed to
me a tinge of contempt in her tone. Then, more
graciously, "We were there a day or two ago.
Papa calls it the finest hotel in the world."

"Particularly as to its service," her father added,
"and to its wines."

It was my turn to laugh now, as I did most
heartily. Then, remembering that they were out
of the joke, I prepared to explain it.

"I beg your pardon," I began; "the fact is that
I — that we — " But at that moment the report
of a cannon startled us all. We were just entering
the village, where the gun had been fired in honor
of the latest successful ascension of the summit.
The horses made a forward plunge, whisked wildly
round the corner, and were then brought up quietly
enough before the door of a small hotel remote
from Worden's and mine. I reached it almost at
the same moment, breathless, but in time to help
Miss Hargrave down. She permitted this small
courtesy, and acknowledging it by a slight inclina-

tion of the head, without so much as a look she swept by me into the house. Her father, following, stopped and turned to me.

"We are grateful to you for your kindness," he said. "I shall hope to see you again one of these days — in Vevey." And he was gone.

In Vevey? Why not in Tokio, or in Khartoum?

In Vevey? Suddenly a light broke in upon me. Reviewing, bit by bit, our fragmentary talk, its constraint was all accounted for. Misinformed at our first meeting through their coachman's gossip, they had taken me for a servant. My own words, as chance willed it, far from disproving this, had strengthened the case against me. To Miss Letty Hargrave I was no more, no less than the second butler of the Three Crowns.

I posted back to Worden in a rage, and hastily told him the story. His delight was immeasurable.

"After all you're not unlike one. It's delicious."

"I can't agree with you."

"Why on earth should you care a copper? You will never see these people any more. By the way, who are they?"

"The Hargraves, — father and daughter."

"The Hargraves!" Then there was a pause, so long that I looked up; but he only drummed upon the table and added, "Ah! indeed."

"Did you ever hear of them?" I asked.

"Yes; I have heard of them."

"Is the old man a general?"

" General, no! He served for a week or so in the Northern army, as a major at the most. Yes, that's it, — Major Hargrave."

" What else can you tell me ? "

" Very little. He's an idle old beggar, living on his means. His house has a high stoop and a brown-stone front. Do you want the number of the street ? I have n't it by me ; but as it's a street in New York we may be sure that it has one. The daughter, — well, you 've seen her."

I sighed, then laughed. My position in the matter was somewhat ludicrous.

" I can't say much for Miss Hargrave's discernment," said I.

" Don't be harsh with her. At night all cats are gray. Had you made now that little speech about your heart —"

" What speech ? "

" Why, you flung it after her down the Villeneuve road, — your heart, I mean, — how many days ago ? "

" Pish! " I cried impatiently. " She's pretty, but she's — well — obtuse."

" Good honest talk! " said Worden. " Stick to it. While you have been masquerading for her benefit, I have been devising means to make your last impressions of Chamouni agreeable. Listen, and forget her. One woman will be as good as another — or as bad — when you come to my age."

" She is forgotten. Go on, patriarch! "

With all the contemptible ardor of a tourist, Worden, in my absence, had actually planned an expedition, and a long one, to a rock-bound slope, high up among the glaciers, called the Jardin.

"It will take us ten hours, or twelve, at most," said he.

"An all day's journey, and on foot," I answered doubtfully. "Where is the Jardin?"

He found it impossible to tell me in words, but taking from one of his pockets a scrap of paper he made upon that a rough diagram of the spot and its approaches.

"It will be a hard pull," I objected.

"Nonsense. Women do it frequently, I am told. Where is your enthusiasm?"

It is hardly necessary to say that I had opposed his scheme from diplomatic motives only, to avoid bearing the burden of it in case things went wrong. It was accordingly arranged that, if the weather were fine, we should attempt the excursion on the following day at an early hour. Upon going to bed that night, I found in my pocket Worden's diagram, which I had unconsciously carried off. As I studied for a moment the blurred lines of his drawing, I noticed a peculiar tint in the paper, and turned it over, wondering how he came by it. On the reverse was written : —

Don't go yet.

Olga Andréevna.

I perceived then that I held in my hand a part of one of Worden's pale-blue telegrams, — an important part, since it bore the sender's name, which was that of our old acquaintance the Russian princess.

"Oho!" thought I, as I wrapped the drapery of my couch about me. "Monsieur the butler-in-chief is himself a diplomatist. It suits him to stay on a little longer; and to lull my suspicions, to keep me in good humor he has racked his brains. The mountain has labored and brought forth its mouse. Worden has invented the Jardin."

But neither in the pleasant dreams to which I then lay down, nor in my subsequent waking hours could I conceive why the Princess Olga should wish at this particular moment to detain him, nor why he, who commonly chafed at all restraint like a stubborn horse, should now submit to be detained. Could it be that she — ? No, the princess had a husband somewhere, I believed, — an ill-favored thing, as Touchstone puts it, but her own. And there had been no semblance of a sheep's-eye, however faint, on her part or on Worden's.

The next day and the next it poured in torrents. Of course we stayed at home; Worden refusing to put even so much as his nose out of doors. We devoted ourselves to chess, and I was checkmated so many times in succession that Worden inquired satirically if I would not prefer to try some game that I knew how to play. Then he was beaten badly, and while my spirits rose he shut up the board and said it was stupid sport after all. Your fine player at anything, one observes, must always win.

Toward the close of the second day I went out for a lonely walk in the rain; but the storm was really over. Broken patches of cloud went scurrying by, revealing rosy light behind them. Somewhere at a lower level of the world there was a sunset.

" To-morrow will be marvellous," said Franz, when I returned, splashed with mud from head to foot. " One day in a thousand!"

" To-morrow, then, the Jardin!" I replied.

" Did you meet anybody in your walk?" demanded Worden.

" No one," said I; " not even the Hargraves."

" 'Not even' is good," he retorted. " I don't trust you out of sight. To-morrow, perhaps, you'll be engaged to her."

" Was it for that," I asked, " that you invented the Jardin?" He looked at me sharply. I think he knew that I meant more than my words did; but he pursued the subject no farther.

The dawn was cloudless as the Swiss had predicted. Though we were up betimes, the peaks got the start of us, lifting sublimely above the lingering night their fresh, unblemished faces. The valley, still asleep, lay dark and cold, chilling us with heavy breaths of vapor. We three seemed to be the only human creatures stirring in it. But the

Arve was awake and boisterous; and everywhere we heard the song of birds. Halfway up the Montanvert we met the perfect day, and watched it stride down below us to greet the meadows and the châlets, one by one. Then, coming out upon the shore of the Mer de Glace, we turned from the beaten track that leads straight across its frozen waves; and following the mountain crest for some distance, we descended to the glacier by means of *Les Ponts,* — a series of small ledges, each of which affords a foothold with little room to spare. This passage, though not dangerous, absorbs one's thought; here, in one of his chamois-leaps, Worden contrived to break his colored eye-glasses, informing us of the mishap profanely. His loss was somewhat serious, for in spite of all that Franz could urge, he had refused to wear a veil; and the ice-glare already dazzled us. He would have leisure for repentance, but I was too busy in crossing the ugly crevasse below him to tell him so. In a few minutes more we had passed the one small peril of our journey, and our course stretched away before us up the central portion of the glacier, over a field of ice almost unbroken.

We walked on toward the heart of this vast solitude, where man finds himself swiftly dwarfed into insignificance by the sight of Nature at her fiercest and grandest, — shut in on all sides by an insurmountable barrier, the splintered points of the Aiguilles. No two are alike, and all are terrible.

Their deep ravines overflow with jagged ice pressing
forward into the field, and their shining surfaces of
rock lead down to instant death upon their own
fragments, — the high, loose walls of the moraines.
The ice beneath assumes strange shapes, — now
regular, as if a skilful hand had formed them, now
distorted and unnatural, more fantastic than bar-
barism itself. There is no roundness, no softness
of vegetation. It is a land of sharpness, angular-
ity, cold and fearful; except for its color, like
a landscape in the moon. But the colors are of
startling beauty. In this shallow glacial pool
lurks a transparent, vivid green, peculiarly its own.
And those well-like shafts near by, as yet unsounded
by any scientific plummet, sink into a blue deeper
and clearer than that we call the blue of heaven.
The lustrous rocky pinnacles have been well compared to spikes of metal, once molten and suddenly
congealed. All things here seem to be of marble
or of copper, with all the cunning processes of
alchemy at work in them.

"Beware of the *moulins!*" cried Franz, pointing
toward a small hole down which a surface rivulet
went roaring away, drowning itself in savage music.
"They are dangerous; one would not desire to step
into them." Just then we heard a sharper sound,
breaking into a rattle, dying off in reverberations
like a peal of thunder. "An avalanche!" explained the guide. "Look! Another!" Far up
a distant mountain-side we saw a faint trail of icy

smoke, moving so slowly that Worden had time to
turn the field-glass which he carried full upon it.
A minute later came the noise, prolonged as before,
echoing and re-echoing.

"That is fine!" said Worden, under his breath.
So far as I know this was the only word of unquali-
fied approval that he wasted upon Switzerland.
We had come, indeed, into an atmosphere of
exhilaration.

Nevertheless, the old contest of the wind and
the sun went on around us ; and the sun got the
better of it, precisely as he did in Æsop's fable.
His mighty blaze tried more than one of our mortal senses. But when I offered compassionately a
strip of my veil to Worden, he scorned it as though
it had been Cupid's blinder. He took this occasion,
moreover, for a fling at my alpenstock, of which,
thus far, I had found little need. Nothing should
ever induce him to brandish this ornamental
weapon. Did I not feel myself to be a model ex-
cursionist, got up for show ? What had I done
with my personal conductor and my ninety-nine
enrolled companions ? Franz inquired what monsieur was saying, and when I told him, he only
laughed discreetly, and called Worden *un gros
farceur.*

But when we left the ice, and toiled up the yielding granite masses of a steep and treacherous
moraine, the use of the *bâton* became at once apparent. Worden went slipping about, making all

his progress laboriously. At last he fell, and after that he suffered Franz to lend him a hand at the difficult places. Aided by my lighter weight, even more than by my staff, I could have distanced them easily, but purposely lagged behind, satisfied to enjoy my obvious triumph in contemptuous silence. In this order we gradually left behind us the great terminal wall of the Talèfre, and gained at length one of the most important stations of our day's march, — a promontory of solid rock, jutting out grandly into the rough, noiseless sea. Here Franz wished that we should repose ourselves for awhile. And here, in some former age, an enormous boulder stopped to rest in its downward course, and never has gone on. In its shelter a patch of long grass has grown, — grass of the richest green, as soft and fine as though it were the fresh sod of an English lawn, grateful to any eyesight that turns toward it from the scorching waste of the *débris;* doubly grateful, now, to Worden's. He threw himself down there in the shadow of the boulder.

"Un beau point de vue," said Franz. "This, Messieurs, is called the Rock of Béranger: —

> "'Ah ! qu'on aspire de courage
> Dans l'air pur du sommet des monts !'"

Though we did not know it then, he had quoted to us the merry poet of the "Roi d' Yvetot," drawing largely for the lines, no doubt, upon his slender stock in trade. Then he dropped back into prose, and gave us a catalogue of Alpine names, to which I listened with indifference, envying his knowledge less than his nationality that made this prospect an old story to him.

Directly at our feet, but far below them, three huge ice-streams met to form the Mer de Glace, the whole length of which we had just surmounted; and on three sides the ice was hemmed in by the bristling summits told off by Franz so glibly. Above them all Mont Blanc showed us a new face, — a wild and frowning one. No mist veiled it, no shred of cloud crept into the clear blue of the sky. Now and then came the white rush of an avalanche, shouting up to us in tones of thunder, — the only sound, the only movement in all this splendid desolation.

"And where," asked Worden, "is the Jardin?"

"Up there," said Franz, pointing at a high moraine behind us, — "up there and beyond; a trifle of another half-hour or so."

Worden eyed for an instant the formidable wall of rock. "That settles it," he said; "I shall wait for you here."

In vain I urged that this was not all he had come out to see.

"I shall see the rest through your observant eyes," he answered, making, as he spoke, the circuit of the small plateau, to explore a rude stone shelter thrown up under the boulder. "This is my domain. If I am molested, which is most unlikely, I shall take refuge in my dog-kennel, and bar the door."

He limped a little as he came back to us, and frankly admitted that he had bruised his knee in falling. There were no bones broken; amputation would not be necessary, he fancied; he did not care to climb, that was all.

We left him food and drink, therefore, and scrambled on without him. The way was not easy; more than once Franz lowered his stick, and pulled me up by it. At the top we looked back, and saw Worden just where we had left him, smoking his cigar alone. But, as we turned away, Franz stopped to point out to me three other figures farther off upon the Mer de Glace, — mere points of moving darkness, that, while we looked, passed out of sight among the rocks below the boulder.

"They are coming to the Jardin," said Franz. "The day is too fine; we cannot have it to ourselves."

I chuckled at the thought of their speedy encroachment upon Worden's philosophical repose.

"He will take to his tub, and shut them out," I reflected. "Poor Diogenes!"

We found the Glacier du Talèfre ankle-deep with wet snow, through which we floundered to another low moraine, and crossing that, we stood at last on the green slope of a little heart-shaped island, completely enclosed with ramparts like a citadel.

A spring bubbled up at our feet. Bright Alpine flowers of strange hues nodded and sparkled in the grass. I thought the breeze had blown one from its stalk; but the color darted here and there with a motion of its own, — it was a butterfly. No wonder that its discoverer had named this place the Garden.

We sat down to rest, to eat and drink away the time. Then Franz curled himself up like a marmot, and went to sleep; while I watched the avalanches, until the long silences between them grew oppressive, bringing me a shuddering sense of loneliness. The very air felt too pure for humanity with all its faults and passions. Voices! It was a relief to hear them. The other party must be very near. In a few moments a guide peered over the wall, and then came down, bringing with him no less a person than Major Hargrave.

He greeted me in civil surprise, while Franz shook himself awake and hobnobbed with the guide.

"And the rest of your party?" said I. "We thought there were three of you."

"Oh, yes; my daughter. She had enough of it, and is waiting below at the other halting-place."

"Alone?"

"Yes. We are only three."

"But — alone?" I repeated.

"Of course," he answered, laughing. "Why not? There are no wild beasts, I believe, and no banditti."

12

Unhappy Worden! He had really imprisoned himself, then, at the sound of their voices.

The major's luncheon was now produced, and with it a bottle of Rüdesheimer, from which he filled a glass for me. He looked somewhat vexed when I declined to drink with him.

" I have lunched already," I explained.

" A glass more or less is nothing," he urged. " But I suppose you prefer the native wines. Every man to his taste. Which, now, do you call your best one ? "

" I have never compared the Swiss wines."

He stared at me in silent wonder. " I see," he said, at length ; " Swiss grapes are like prophets, — for exportation only."

" Perhaps. I really don't know."

He grew more and more perplexed, while I quietly enjoyed his confusion.

" May I ask where you learned English ? " he demanded abruptly.

" Oh, yes ; in a land where it is spoken fluently, — the United States of America."

" Is it possible ? But I understood — "

" That I was in the service of the Three Crowns. Quite the reverse. I am a good Yankee, but I can't 'keep a hotel!' Perhaps because I have never tried."

He burst into a loud laugh, and begged me a thousand pardons ; when I told him the whole story, he begged ten thousand more. Then we buried our little hatchet in his Rhenish wine.

"It was your own fault, after all," he said amiably. "You spoke French so well."

I had heard him try to speak it, and could therefore appreciate the true value of his compliment; but I thanked him none the less.

"And you can read it too, of course?"

"Well, yes; a little."

"Then help me out with this," he said, unfolding a newspaper, and letting his voice fall into a whisper. "It came by post yesterday; from whom I can't imagine. These long words puzzle me, and I could not ask my daughter. I did not like to let her know."

The French journal, printed at Geneva, was three days old. In a long letter from the regular correspondent at Vevey, I found a marked passage recounting the loss of an American tourist near the summit of the Mer de Glace. He had gone out to walk alone and had not returned. There could be no doubt of his sad fate, for untiring search had brought to light an alpenstock with his veil tied to it, at a point known as the Rock of Béranger. The man's description followed, last of all his name. The story was told in a florid style, with many mournful interjections; and it was signed, "Trois Couronnes." I caught its purport at a glance, and was thus enabled to translate it gravely, word for word, in a firm voice. This feat, however, was more than difficult, for the description and the name were Worden's.

"Yes, yes; I thought so," sighed Major Hargrave, as I read on to the end. I was just preparing to laugh at him, when he grew strangely confidential, after the manner of your good American, who comes upon a sympathetic compatriot in some lonely corner of the world.

"It is terrible," he whispered. "I hardly dare to tell you what I fear — and yet — "

"You may trust me. What is it that you fear ? "

"A case of suicide," said Major Hargrave, turning white at the word. "The man was dead in love, — desperately so. I happen to know it. He has killed himself. It is as if I knew that too."

For one instant my face must have been whiter than his own. What if this nameless, petty fiend, this printer's devil, with cunning prescience had lied like truth? What if Worden, desperate to folly, had dismissed me that shining morning to take his own life, and had chosen for his fatal deed, by a strange chance, the very spot the lie had branded? He *was* dead in love; I knew that; but he was not a fool. And so the color came back into my face, and I laughed at the doleful look in Major Hargrave's.

"Don't laugh!" he cried imploringly. "To me it is a most distressing matter. He was a capital fellow. You could not laugh if you had known him."

Not know my fellow-traveller? At this absurd suggestion I only laughed the more. But the major lost his temper, and turning red as a turkey-cock, he shook the lying letter in my face.

"Damn it, sir, do you call that a joke?"

"Excuse me; I can't help it. Your dead man is n't dead; that's all."

"Not dead?"

"Dead in love, yes; but in the flesh, alive and well. He has turned hermit, and gone into a retreat. Present address, the Rock of Béranger."

"Where is that, in the Devil's name?"

"Why, the great boulder, — the halting-place there, below us."

"What! Where my daughter —"

Then Major Hargrave turned from red to purple, and laughed till he woke the echoes like an avalanche, — till the very guides, without knowing why, joined in the laugh, and prolonged the echo; and I too, but for cause. Worden loved in vain. The major knew it; well and good, but how? Why should he take my companion's small affair of the heart so seriously and so merrily unless it concerned his own companion, Miss Letty Hargrave?

I asked no questions, and he told me nothing. As we came out into the land of snow, his mind wandered off into a maze of conjecture regarding the origin of the tale in print. I had found my own clew to that, but I kept it to myself. At the green plateau we found Worden and Miss Hargrave chatting pleasantly like old friends. She smiled when she saw me, and at last we were introduced.

But she made no allusion to the stupid mistake concerning my identity, of which she had been the victim; perhaps because she thought me too dull to notice the difference between reserve and cordiality.

While we talked, Worden and Major Hargrave exchanged confidences with much suppressed hilarity. " I assure you I knew nothing of it," I heard Worden say. The guides called us to order. We looked our last at the waning splendor of the glaciers, along which the shadows were slowly lengthening; and then we all came down together.

Worden, still limping though not disabled, dropped behind with the major, leaving Miss Hargrave entirely to me. She was all charm and sweetness now, with that air of bewitching coquetry which had impressed me at the very first. Without vanity I may record my conviction that she tried her best to captivate me that day. For had I been a monster of deformity I believe she would have done the same. Luckily for my peace of mind I could not forget that she had just mistaken me for a servant, and she left me as she found me, irresponsive. But under other circumstances I should have gone to bed that night madly in love with her, — and much she would have cared. She, of all women, had the least right to such a conquest then. But what of that ? Your brilliant blue-and-gold macaw, to the last gasp, will allure you with a pretty attitude, only to turn and rend you. You cannot change its nature. Macaws are made so.

It was late when we got back to our hotel; but I followed Worden to his room, went in after him, and shut the door.

"Will you be kind enough to tell me," I demanded, "what all this means?"

"To the best of my ability. But first, perhaps, I ought to tell you —" He hesitated.

"What?" I asked impatiently.

"That I am engaged to Miss Hargrave."

"Since when?" I stammered, too much startled for congratulation.

"Since this morning. We agreed to let you know."

I quoted Franz, and, through him, Béranger.

> "'Ah! qu'on aspire de courage
> Dans l'air pur du sommet des monts!'

For this, then, you invented the Jardin."

"No," he said, laughing. "It wasn't in the programme. After you left me, I fled into the hut at the sound of voices. When all was quiet, and I thought I was alone again, I came out. To my amazement there was Letty — Miss Hargrave — crying like a child over a letter."

"A letter?"

"Yes, — or rather its enclosure; half a newspaper column, describing my awful death, — a duplicate of that the major showed you."

"She knew of it, then?"

"The writer took good care of that."

"I see. And so—"

"So she screamed at the sight of me, and I thought she would have fallen. I caught her, I believe. And then—odd, wasn't it?"

"Very. Your lead of trumps has been fully justified."

"Don't be an ass," he cried indignantly. "I didn't lead. I only followed suit."

"What? That obituary notice was not your work?"

"No; I tell you. I knew nothing of it, absolutely nothing. All I knew was this."

And he handed me the following letter:—

CHER ANIMAL,—Ask her again, and you will get her. She has refused you once, twice, you will say, a dozen times; I care not how many. Some women are like that. And this one loves you; I am sure of it. So I have telegraphed you again to wait in Chamouni. Disobey me at your peril. In proof, I venture upon a small experiment. It shall do no harm; perhaps it shall do good. I pray for this, for you and for myself. It would be such joy for me to accomplish this good action, since there are not too many to remember in my life. Be discreet therefore, and if I go wrong instead of right, forgive

Your best—or worst—of friends,

OLGA ANDRÉEVNA.

I looked at Worden. If any man on earth could be called completely happy, it was surely he.

"The princess is adorable," I said. "My dear old man, with all my heart I congratulate you."

With what a vengeance Time can turn his tables! She, who led him such a dance, now sits at his clumsy feet, and has no thought that is not his. He loves her too in his own way, which is a shade less devotional than hers. But that you know him, you might almost reproach him with indifference. Who, not knowing him, would ever guess how much she made him suffer, how freely he forgave her on the instant, putting all but love away? And I, who longed to climb, now hobble painfully, content if I can hold my own on level ground. Rheumatism the doctor calls it; but I know better, it is gout. I know also that the rare blue we call the blue of heaven is but an aqueous evaporation. Ah! were all to do again, the upper air should never tempt me. I too would lie down and rest most gladly under the Rock of Béranger.

MAESTRO AMBROGIO.

IN a certain narrow street of Florence, near Andrea del Sarto's house and the Annunziata's choir, where with maimed rites the mortal part of the poor painter *senza errori* was hurried under the pavement, there lived in the latter half of the fifteenth century a learned doctor whose name and titles history is scarcely able to recall. Yet the young Andrea may have known him; and the illustrious Leonardo, called Da Vinci, wise in many things and ennobling all with a touch rarer than the golden one of fable, was surely numbered among his friends. But the doctor led a life of deep seclusion, indifferent to the storms of party strife, to plot and insurrection, battles and murders, the tyrant's yoke, the tyrant's favor. His four gray walls sheltered him from the summer's heat, the winter's cold; his little garden caught from the sunlight all the colors of the prism in roses, wild pomegranates, and oleanders. The laboratory behind it held his store of manuscripts, his retorts and crucibles, his furnace and his bellows, all the apparatus needed for experiments which so absorbed him that he seldom went out into the bustling streets. He had but one thought, one purpose, — to make some vast discovery which should benefit the human race; and as he was human too, one may imagine that his ambition went a little farther, coupling with the glorious result his own name, and immortalizing that. Undoubtedly he longed and hoped to live forever in men's hearts; to have his ashes consecrated in a gilded shrine, surmounted by a marble bust, — a goal of pilgrimage. Alas! None knows where he lies buried. You may find his house to-day in the Via del Mandorlo, — his laboratory has been turned into a stable; the roses still run riot in his garden, and the snails still nibble at their leaves; but the last of many tenants, treading the very paths he trod, will smile and tell you that the property has been in his own family from time immemorial, and that no such man ever lived and died there as Maestro Ambrogio.

He was a bachelor of course, and had come to that time of life when a man is neither young nor old, and when a few additional years work little change in him. His figure was slender and well-proportioned; but his shoulders had the scholar's stoop, his thin face the hungry look of an ascetic; the bright blue eyes in it seemed younger than the rest of him; for contrary to all custom of the day, he went unshorn and unshaven, and his brown hair, streaked with gray, mingled with the untrimmed beard that swept over his breast, muffling him like a disguise. He wore habitually the Florentine *lucco*, or long robe of black serge, familiar to the world through Dante's portraits; and with this, the hood-like civic bonnet of the same material. These garments, in spite of his absorbing pursuits, were always of the most scrupulous neatness; while his hands were marvellously white and slender, fine, delicate, like the hands of a noble. But the man's nobility of nature found its best expression in his voice, which was low and clear, never querulous, never raised in anger, of surpassing gentleness and patience in all its tones; so that he who heard it for the first time stood spell-bound in respectful silence, as though the speech were half divine, and its simple phrases the utterance of an oracle.

Few, however, beyond the narrow limits of his household, ever heard the voice of Maestro Ambrogio. His one servant, an old peasant woman from the mountains of the Mugello, stood between him and all the cares and worries of the outer world. Monna Modesta was well known in the quarter. It was she who went to market for him, who knew the worth of a plump fowl, and was ready to pay just that and no more; above all, who kept her master's house in the wonderful and incredible state of cleanliness noted in chronicles of the time. But only the house; she was never allowed to pass beyond the garden, to profane the dust of the laboratory with her vulgar hands. This, to one of her instincts, was a positive and constant grief. With tears in her eyes she bade the saints witness that her master's good was all she had at heart, and that dust was the insidious foe of all mankind; yet Maestro Ambrogio remained a very pig for obstinacy, as she declared. The laboratory and its contents were never to be touched; he and his young pupil, the noble signor Gentile Morelli, alone could enter it; even its small windows, high above her head, must not be scoured. This last command was hardly to be borne, and for a time she persistently disobeyed it,—climbing the trellis in her master's absence, removing dead leaves from the sills, polishing the leaded panes; and since she could not open them, peering within, defiantly, upon a group of broken jars stored away on a neglected shelf and half buried in cobwebs, through which the wicked old spiders eyed her with indifference. Beyond these evidences of pestilential disorder she saw dimly, in the feeble glow of the furnace, a confusion of utensils whose very names were unknown to her. And one day when there was more light than usual, she also discerned the outlines of a splendid alabaster chest, of great size and carved in high relief, but sadly stained and blackened. In her simple ignorance she took this for a linen-coffer, and longed to have it removed and cleansed and restored to its proper uses under her careful supervision. The good soul little dreamed that this sculptured wonder had been designed merely to hold what she most despised; namely, dust. For it was an Etruscan sarcophagus, found long ago by her master in his mountain vineyard near Gubbio, and by him brought down to Florence with reverent care, for the sake of its principal figure,— a young girl, recumbent in the marble, but life-like, as if a touch would rouse her; the portrait, no doubt, of the dead unknown whose ashes Maestro Ambrogio still treasured, undisturbed.

Monna Modesta, wise in her small way, applied to herself that proverb of her nation which prizes the ounce of discretion above the pound of knowledge. As a matter of course, she gave her master no cause to suspect that she had climbed the trellis to look upon these things, prudently resolving to pry into them no more. But she continued to sound the praises of order and her own devotion to it on all possible occasions; with righteous thanks that she was not as others were, uplifting her standard at the gate of the enemy's citadel, to wage fierce warfare upon the insects of the garden, where not so much as a leaf was permitted to fall unperceived; while the student Gentile, having daily access to the precincts from which she was so rigorously excluded, daily grew in her disfavor. She looked upon him as a poor misguided creature, aiding and abetting her master in practices that were, to say the least, unwholesome, and that did no good to anybody, so far as honest folk could see.

Toward the close of a lovely day when the long Italian summer was nearly gone, Monna Modesta sat spinning and considering deeply many things. She had moved her wheel into a sunny corner of the garden, and the grateful warmth reminded her that winter was not far off, and that winter, at her age, was to be dreaded. She must go to market in the morning and get the better of old Niccolò, who was a rascal at heart, and would cheat her if he could. The thought caused her wheel to rattle angrily. The world's prevailing wickedness made duty doubly hard; the wicked seemed to thrive and flourish, while for the good, life was a long contention, with palsy at the end. The breeze shook down some dead leaves from the rose trained above her head. Yes, autumn had already come; and what would befall her master if the winter should be her last? He could never take care of himself; he must inevitably become the prey of thieves. She sighed, and the wheel stopped turning; the dry leaves rustled under foot, but she did not stoop for them.

A key grated in the lock of the laboratory door. The sound passed unheeded, and her master's presence was first made known to her by his shadow on the garden-path. The wheel resumed its work, but quite unconsciously she sighed again.

"Why do you sigh, my good Modesta?" asked Maestro Ambrogio.

"The winter is at hand, my master. I feel its breath already, and I am old."

"*Madre mia*, with such nimble fingers!" returned the doctor, as he watched the whirring wheel. "There is no winter in your blood."

"Eh, Signor, the candle burns low; a puff will put it out. And who then will look after you? Not the miserable Gentile, that insect, who knows less of the world's ways than would fill a snail-shell. The house that has no woman in it is a ruined house, Signor. You must marry, that I may die content."

"Death will come," said the doctor, gravely; "but yesterday you did not fear it. And it is only one day nearer now. You talk of winter too before its time. See, above your head, there is a rose."

"The last," she answered; "to pick that would bring ill luck upon the house. Master, do not touch it, I pray you."

But the rose was already plucked, and as the doctor held it out to her, its petals fell apart in the hollow of his hand. To Monna Modesta this was the worst of omens, and as if to confirm her superstitious fancy, a violent gust of the autumn breeze shook every twig in the garden, and raised a cloud of dust about their feet. The small whirlwind passed them by in a moment; but she had spoken truly, — there was winter in its breath.

"Keep the rose, Signor," she said reproachfully;

" for death has overtaken it. Is not this a warning? Make haste to choose your wife, and choose her well, Maestro Ambrogio."

The doctor smiled and pointed at the door of his laboratory.

" My wife is there," said he, lightly. " She is wise and gentle and forgiving, with no complaints and no harsh words. She is always young, always beautiful; after all these years, would you have me turn against her now, and prove unfaithful ? "

" Has my master lost his senses ? " muttered Monna Modesta. " Of what woman is he speaking ? "

" Of no woman, but of Science," replied the doctor, laughing. " She is the best and sweetest wife in the whole world."

" A fig for her ! " cried the old servant, testily. " Tell me ! Can Science go to market, and choose between an old fowl and a tender chicken ? Can she mind the spit, or sew new hooks upon the robe you wear ? Can she make me young again, or even persuade me that I am not growing old ? Science ! Bah ! Can she turn winter into spring, or bring the dead to life ? "

" Or bring the dead to life ! " The doctor had gone laughing to his work again. But these words made him start; they rang in his ears after the door had closed upon them. He stood grave and silent, far removed in thought from the musty disorder of his workshop, until a sweet perfume, strangely out of place there, recalled him to him-

13

self; it came only from the fading flower, rudely crushed and broken in his hand.

" The last rose," he said, gathering up carefully some of its outer petals that had fallen to the floor. " Will it bring ill luck upon the house ? We shall see, — we shall see ! "

That night Monna Modesta summoned him in vain to supper. She laid the cloth, and sitting down beside it watched and waited, then nodded and dozed over it alone. She awoke at a late hour, to find the food still there, untasted. A light shone in the laboratory; and stealing out into the dark, she climbed the trellis cautiously to the little window and looked down. There sat the doctor before a small brazier filled with glowing embers, turning the leaves of a parchment book in old black-letter. He stopped and sighed ; then, to her astonishment, he flung the fragments of a rose — her rose — into the heart of the hot coals, and fell to reading again in the great book. A cannon-shot would hardly have aroused him from his studies. But she crept back as quietly as she came, in speechless wonder ; went to her bed, slept, and dreamed, still wondering.

In the morning the table stood precisely as she had left it ; her master's bed was empty ; and her honest wrath broke forth upon the head of the student Gentile, who came at his accustomed hour. He was a handsome youth, wearing a cloak of violet silk jauntily draped over his velvet doublet. A

lute was slung across his shoulder. The very ease
and trimness of him carried Monna Modesta's
anger beyond the bounds of reason.

"Here are fine doings truly!" she cried.
"Maestro Ambrogio has had neither food nor sleep
this night. Why was not your splendid laziness
here to help him?" And never listening for his
answer, she went on, —

"Go out and fetch him in to breakfast. I pray
our Gracious Lady that he be not starved already.
If you find him dead, lay it at your own door,
popinjay!"

Maestro Ambrogio looked pale and worn, but
somewhat to her regret, he was not dying of starvation. She pointed at the table with an injured
air.

"It is true," he said, "I have an appetite. But
as you see, my night's work was not unprofitable."

And before seating himself he handed her a
rose.

She knew that none were left in the garden, yet
she turned instinctively to the window; for the
flower was but half open, and seemed to have the
morning freshness in it.

He shook his head and smiled.

"No," he said; "I did not find it there. To
please you, I have restored the dead to life. That
is all."

He was above any wilful deception, before all
human creatures to be trusted; but now she

doubted him, even while she could not help observing that, in size and color, this was the perfect counterpart of the rose so lately reduced to ashes under her too curious eyes.

" Well," he continued, " you will never say sharp things any more about my gentle mistress. Come ! Confess that her work has been complete and wonderful."

" Wonderful ! " repeated Monna Modesta, pressing the rose to her lips that she might conceal her doubts behind it. Then she found it dry and scentless, and she believed him.

But the increased respect with which she now regarded her master had a touch of pity in it, a new tenderness unfelt before. It was plain that he failed to perceive the fatal imperfection of his handiwork ; his air of triumph betrayed conclusively an absolute faith in his own skill. And the old servant could not find the heart to undeceive him, but left his mind clouded with this last illusion, as if she had been dealing with a child. After all the rose without its perfume was a sufficient marvel ; she put it away in water, crossing herself involuntarily, as she did so. While it lived, her wholesome awe of it continued ; she would not even touch the unholy thing again, but when it had faded for the second time, seizing the dried stalk with a pair of tongs, at arm's length, she flung it into the fire ; then raked apart the ashes. They should not kindle into another life through any fault of hers.

Winter came, and with it the first symptoms of the infirmity she feared. Her voice shook in an annoying way, her step grew heavier, her wrinkles deepened; she compared herself to an old witch, when she looked in the glass. Her lightest household care became a burden, even grumbling was an effort. But she toiled and scolded and drove her bargains with unflagging spirit, praying only that death might find her still in the pious fury of her work. She was ready; let this hour be her last, — she wanted no interval of deplorable rest, no sickly folding of the hands.

Her master's future gave her more concern than ever. He had drawn very near, he told her, to that greatest of discoveries which had baffled him so long. But no further hint of his revealed anything of its scope or even of its nature. Vainly, she took the young student into favor, plying him with wine, artfully leading him on to gossip indiscreetly about Maestro Ambrogio's affairs; and gaining only a reluctant admission that Gentile was quite ignorant of the possible result to which their labors tended. He performed his share of them adroitly, by his own showing, and slept soundly each night when they were over. But at his return, he often found that the last day's work had been undone. For day and night his master seemed to toil incessantly, suffering repeated discouragements, but through them all upheld and strengthened by some wild hope that he would not explain.

One morning Gentile presented himself only to
be sent away again. All that day Maestro Ambrogio did no work and spoke no word. Monna Modesta came and went, but he never heeded her
until she made a direct attack upon him with in-
trusive questions, when he shook his head mournfully. His eyes glistened; a tear trickled down
upon his beard; she was sure, then, that his experiments had failed.

"Heaven help us all!" she thought; and clat-
tering off to the neighboring church, she said her
prayers in one of its chapels.

She heard him stirring in the night; he left his
room, his step died away upon the stairs. She followed, but not softly enough, for at the garden
door, in the dark, she found him waiting. She felt
his hand upon her wrist, and drew back, alarmed.
But his reproof was of the gentlest.

"Why do you get up so early? One watcher is
enough to guard my house. Go to your bed, and
sleep; it is the best service you can do me."

She obeyed him silently.

The next day, Maestro Ambrogio recalled his
student. The old hope had revived, informing new
schemes, inducing new tests. And as time passed,
as his problem advanced favorably toward its
mysterious solution, the confidence daily growing
stronger within him shone through his eyes and
gave his face the radiance of youth. He was like
the fortunate lover who believes that some divinity

has alighted upon the earth to walk hand in hand with him forever.

At length, when Monna Modesta imagined that the hour of triumph must be very near, her master, who so rarely stirred abroad, suddenly bade her prepare him for a long journey. In answer to her startled look, he told her that all was well with him; that he had only one venture left to make; but that he dared not run the extreme risk it involved without first consulting the one living man whose judgment could be called infallible. This was a famous Venetian doctor, almost a century old, unimpaired in mind, but far too feeble in body to endure the fatigue of travel, which, therefore, he himself must undertake. He charged her solemnly to admit no one, not even Gentile, to the house during his absence. The laboratory door he locked and sealed, leaving all behind him, apparently, except a scroll of parchment easily to be carried in the hand. The time appointed for departure came; the horse stood at the door, and Maestro Ambrogio lingering upon the threshold gave his last instructions. Then, with a smile, he added, —

" And how shall I reward you for so much fidelity? What shall I bring back from Venice to my constant friend?"

" Ah, Signor, a kind, gentle mistress, — only that. Marry your wife, and bring her back with you."

" A wife, from Venice?" said the doctor, laughing. " Well, who knows ? I have done stranger things. But, remember, I make no promises. God be with you, Modesta ! "

" And with you, Signor. A swift journey, Maestro Ambrogio ! "

So he rode away. For many days there was no sign of him, and she was faithful to her trust. When Gentile demanded news, he found the house barricaded as if for a siege, and was forced to hold indignant parley with Modesta through a wicket in the outer door. She bade him sing to his lute and not to her. The great Leonardo knocked once, faring little better.

" What ! Hast thou yet heard nothing of thy master ? "

" Alas, no, Signor."

" *Misericordia!* Pray Heaven that some sly one of thy sex may not have beguiled him ! "

" Pray Heaven that he be no more a bachelor ; and good day to you, Messer Leonardo."

At last, however, the door swung open for the master's much-desired return. He came, dressed in gay colors, with a light step and smiling face, followed by two serving-men bearing rich apparel, ribbons, silks, and laces, to be unfolded and displayed before Modesta's wondering eyes. She tried to speak, but wanted words.

" What ! No welcome for me ? " he cried merrily. " Yet all is as you wished it. I come in my wedding garments ; are they not well chosen ? "

" Heaven be praised for all its mercies! You have grown young again. But the bride, Signor ? "

" She will follow. Prepare a chamber for her and for these things."

" Eh, the waste of money! Look at that brocade ! What great lady have you married ? These trappings are for a princess; how is it that your wife will wear them ? "

" They are not fine enough. Wait, and you will see."

She set the house in order with much nervous apprehension. How should she make room for these new fineries ? There was no chest fit to hold them, except, perhaps, the splendid marble one hidden away in her master's workshop; but she dared not ask him for that. Well, it mattered little ; no doubt the new mistress would bring a retinue of servants to undo any humble work of hers ; they would overrule her, — she would count for nothing; that, of course, was the fate of age, and she must accept it cheerfully ; she must bid them all good-night, and let the past to which she belonged enshroud her in its friendly shadows. All would be for the best, that promised a long and happy future to Maestro Ambrogio.

Thus Modesta dealt with her misgivings. But the new mistress did not come. Again the doctor buried himself in the laboratory, and pursued his dreary studies. To all inquiries about his wife he replied that she was still to be expected; but he

fixed no day, no hour. Then, fearing that the
great lady might take them by surprise in the
night, she slept with a lighted lamp near her bedside, to wake continually, and strain her ears at
the faintest sound. But her master discovered
this, and rebuked her almost sternly for excess of
zeal. So she resumed her former habits, asked no
more questions, left events to wait upon themselves, the stars to rise and set as they would, un-
noted; till the winter had worn away.

The doctor's cellar contained a few bottles of old
wine, lying there in wait for rare occasions. One
evening of the early spring-time, he brought out
from this dusty ambush a small flask, and uncork-
ing it with deliberation, he called for glasses. All
that day he had been in a state of feverish disturbance, and his hand shook now. The golden liquor
leaped and sparkled in a most inviting way; and
Monna Modesta, yielding readily to temptation,
took the glass he offered; likewise a second, which
he pressed upon her. She wondered what silent
toast they could be drinking, — for this, assuredly,
was a kind of ceremonial. But she had grown too
old for such indulgences. The wine made her
strangely drowsy. Was there mischief in it? Why
had she taken so much? Why had she touched it
at all? She went to her room, repenting of this
childish folly, and slept profoundly the sleep of
childhood throughout the night, far on into the
morning hours.

The flood of sunshine to which she woke gave its own startling evidence of time unduly wasted; but even this reproachful glare had failed to act upon her sluggish senses. That worthless insect, Gentile, clamored at her door; and his voice rang with delight at the detection of her grievous lapse in duty.

"Modesta! Monna Modesta! Wake, and find your wits! My master's wife has come from Venice, and no one stirs a finger to receive her. Do you sleep all night and all day too?"

"Beast!" she cried in a passion. "Have done with bellowing, and mend your manners. When I sleep at all, it is with my eyes open. Go back and tell them I'll come presently."

Below, in the state apartment long ago made ready for this festal day, the old servant found Maestro Ambrogio in his brightest colors, but formal and solemn as a sentinel; and there too on a low couch lay the noble lady, sleeping.

How young, how fair she was! As sweet, as simple in her beauty as the Virgin of the Annunziata's shrine! Yet these soft features were a-glow with life, these full, red lips were not divine, but exquisitely human. About her head she had bound a veil, through which her heavy coils of hair showed gleams of reddish gold; and she had put on the rich, brocaded garment brought from Venice, worth a fortune in *quattrini*. It seemed, in truth, not fine enough; it should have been sown with jewels.

But her only ornament was a slender golden thread of curious design, clasping one wrist.

She moved a little, smiling in her sleep; and the smile was mysterious, unaccountable, perplexing as the smile of archaic sculpture, — with something of malice in it, as though the thought behind, concealed rather than expressed, were not unmixed with evil. So the sirens must have smiled when the bark foundered, and the poor mariner went unresisting to his death, happy in that inexplicable joy, — perhaps exultant even, — with the look upon his face that Maestro Ambrogio's now wore.

"See!" he murmured. "Was not this worth years of loneliness? Could one have better fortune, even in his dreams?"

But Modesta trembled with a vague distrust, as if some disaster were impending. The smile was hateful to her.

"Ah, Signor," she sighed, "is that my mistress?"

Her master had already turned away, rapt in his dream, and sheltered by it from outward influences.

"Iovina!" he called softly. "Iovina!"

Then the sleeper woke. He caught her hands and kissed them, drawing her toward him from the couch, folding in his arms the lovely presence that had the smile of absence in it still.

The light in her clear gray eyes, however, was reassuring. Her voice too was a pleasant one, though it uttered strange words which Modesta could not understand; but her master answered them in the same tongue. The new mistress looked wonderingly yet not unkindly upon the faithful servant. It appeared from what was said that she had come alone, with no train of attendants to be taught their duties. Modesta would have her own way to all intents and purposes; would still reign supreme in the market-place, be Monna Modesta, *padrona della casa*, to them all. This cheering reflection did away with presentiments for the time being. The household affairs went on that day as usual; only that sometimes in the pauses of work Modesta shook her head, and whispered to herself doubtfully, —

"Iovina! I do not like it; it is a pagan name."

She shook her head in the same discontented fashion over many things that happened in the following days. As might have been expected, her master led, at first, a life of complete infatuation. Then he resumed his studies, but with half a heart, interrupting them under the smallest pretext to dance attendance on the languid lady whose slave he had become. To show his wife a flower in the garden, to read her a line of Tuscan verse that should give her in one breath a better knowledge of his love and of his language, were tasks of more importance than any prescribed to him in those ponderous books of his. This, of course, was commendable and proper; one pardons, nay, exacts some such parade of weakness in the

manners of a bridegroom. It was in the attitude
of her mistress that Modesta found the first cause
for complaint. Clearly, Maestro Ambrogio's devotion was wholly wasted; day by day he squan-
dered it, like the money woven into the embroidered
garments worn by his foreign princess, who either
had no heart to give him in return, or had chosen
to withhold her gift. Her thoughts seemed always
on the wing. The dragon-fly, darting to and fro
among the leaves, could win her smile as easily as
the poor man's fondest word. She was no happier
for his approach; her steel-gray eyes never looked
upon him tenderly. At what, then, was she always
smiling? At him, perhaps; not with him, surely.
For all his kindness must have failed to touch her,
since she took it so impassively, — sometimes, indeed, as if she hardly knew that he was at her side.

Ah! All men were alike, and all were fools!
It needed no spark of feeling to bewitch them,
not even a pretence of it. Here was Gentile, now,
openly worshipping this same idol with eager eyes.
A stray glance from her would upset him for a
whole day. And Messer Leonardo too! At the
first sight of her face his admiration burst forth
in a torrent of superlatives. She smiled upon him;
he laughed, and talked of other things; but his
eyes never left her. He came again, and asked
that she might sit to him; and when permission
was refused, almost on his knees, he begged, implored Maestro Ambrogio to grant it. The smile

haunted him, he said, impelling him to paint it from memory if not from life; its perfect beauty existed for no day, no generation, but must be fixed and made imperishable for all to know until the end of time. Without this attempt, he should hold himself false to the divine art he served; and with all the success he had achieved, with laurels heaped on laurels in the future, hereafter ages would hold him forever miserable, if this duty to the world went unfulfilled, if, for want of means or want of inspiration, he had failed on earth to perpetuate that faultless smile.

These entreaties in the end prevailed. The painter began upon his first sketch, — a drawing in red chalk, at which he worked for days, but only to destroy it. The pose was wrong, he explained, he must try another; and this too came to nothing. He lamented bitterly his own incompetence. Never had subject thwarted him like this; always the look he wanted was not there. That elusive smile played tricks with him; its lovely lines would not be caught, but changed their places before he could reproduce them. How to do her justice? How to accomplish what he already feared would prove impossible? To control that look awhile, he must control the sitter's mind; he must have music, some sweet, delightful strain to charm her into subjection to his will. So Gentile brought his lute only too readily, and played to them, while a new drawing was begun, and all went well with it.

But all went far from well with Maestro Ambrogio. Of late he had grown moody and despondent, — most unlike himself. And now, to-day, he left his furnace to pace aimlessly back and forth in one of the garden-paths, — that farthest away from the great hall of the house, where the painter had set up his easel near an open window, through which Gentile's music and even Messer Leonardo's progress could be followed. For now and then, the master spoke a word of satisfaction, in his own encouragement; he had found the way at last; here was success indeed. But the master of the house only sighed when he heard this, and his step grew heavier and more uncertain, as though a leaden-clog were dragging at his heels.

What weight of sorrow thus depressed him? Old Modesta knew him too well, had watched him too closely not to have divined it. All was plain enough. The scales had fallen from his eyes; he had come to doubt the wisdom of his choice, to distrust the smile of the enchantress, and with reason. In one fatal cast, rashly made, he had flung away his life; and now he repented his rashness. The poor serving-woman, who loved him better than she loved herself, looked at him and longed to help him, but could not find the way. What comfort had she to offer? If she spoke, what good would her words do? This, — that he would be forced to answer them; and if he did not speak, his heart would surely break. So, praying

Heaven to guide her, she went out and stopped him in his walk.

"My master," she began; "never have I seen you so unhappy. What is it now that troubles you?"

He stared at her with shining eyes, dry and tearless.

"Nothing," he answered, — "nothing."

The tears were in her eyes. "Oh, my poor master!" she sighed mournfully. But he brushed by her, and was gone again, muttering to himself.

"My wife!" she heard him say.

Then there came a shout of triumph, and the painter dashed out upon them with the drawing in his hand.

"See!" he cried. "I have surpassed myself. Who will dare to tell me this is not worthy of her?"

In that glowing moment of success he had no thought beyond his work. The doctor took the paper, while Leonardo, passing behind him and leaning upon his shoulder, failed to note with what trouble he regarded it.

Modesta looked on silently. They made a picture in themselves against a background of the vine-leaves, as if they had been posed for embodiments of light and darkness. Light gleamed in the painter's rose-hued silken mantle, in his flushed cheek, his joyous eyes. He was all aflame. In the other all was clouded, cold.

But the hand of genius has a strength that can-

not be resisted; and it held her master now.
Slowly the light illumined him. His face brightened, until it reflected the painter's look of
exultation.

"It is wonderful!" he whispered.

"Caro mio!" said that other master there behind him. "This is a fortunate hour for us both;
we must not let it slip. I will go home and get
my colors; then make the portrait, — finish it,
while the light lasts. Think, *amico:* this day's
work will hang upon some wall in Florence ages
hence, when we are only memories; and all the
painters of the world will bow before it. They
will say: 'See how one brushmark, tracing out a
woman's smile, gave poor Da Vinci his undying
fame! Look at Leonardo's masterpiece, — Iovina,
Maestro Ambrogio's wife!'"

"Yes," returned the doctor, eagerly. "The colors, — bring the colors, noble Leonardo."

The painter hurried off, catching as he went a
note of laughing music, and singing his own song
to it. For in the house Gentile's lute played on.

Then, as the doctor listened, his face grew dull
and grave again. The old dark thought possessed
him wholly. The lovely drawing slipped from his
hand, falling face downward in the earth. He let
it lie there, and turning away, he flung himself
upon one of the garden-benches, hiding his own
face.

The silent witness, whom he had forgotten, now

forgot herself. Overcome with his despair, she knew neither what she said nor what she did, but rushing forward, knelt beside him, and poured out her inmost soul in a flood of unconsidered words.

"Master, why did you marry her? She has brought ruin upon the house; she cares for nothing that is good; she never goes to church, never says a prayer; she is a pagan, a demon. How has she ensnared you?"

"Modesta, Modesta! What words are these?"

"I cannot help it, — I cannot bear it longer. Why did you go so far to bring her home? She is not like other women. *Maestro mio*, she has no heart, no tenderness. She is like the flower that sprung out of the ashes, — beautiful, without its fragrance."

She had risen nearly to her feet in her excitement; but Maestro Ambrogio now caught her by the wrist, and forced her back upon her knees.

"What do you mean?" he asked.

"Forgive me, Master; I forgot — "

"Speak!" he continued sharply. "What flower do you mean?"

"The rose," replied Modesta, — "the dead rose that seemed to live again. Signor, it was not life, for life has sweetness in it. And she has none, — she has no feeling, no kindness in her. She is like the rose."

As though the woman had stabbed him to the heart, he released her with a moan of anguish.

"Oh, had I known!" he cried in a broken voice. "Of all men that ever breathed I am the most pitiable. It is true,—it is true. She is like the rose."

A light breeze caught the fallen paper, which fluttered to his feet. He stooped for the master's handiwork, considered it one moment, then tore it up, and gave it to the winds again,—not angrily, but deliberately, with a look and gesture of the deepest sorrow.

Modesta nodded approvingly; then her eyes flashed. He should do more than this; such calm submission was intolerable.

"Listen!" she cried. "My lady must have music. What cares she for your unhappiness? The boy amuses her, and she smiles upon him. Ay! Go on with it; play and sing to her, do!"

The words were hardly spoken when the music stopped. The doctor rose and moved slowly toward the house without an answer to Modesta, who, accepting the silent rebuke, followed him meekly, but only to the window.

The lute lay upon the floor. There was the painter's seat, there his empty easel; and beyond, where he had posed her, half reclined the lovely figure he longed to make immortal. But now Gentile knelt beside her, drew her face down to his and kissed it; and she permitted this. She did not draw away; the golden ornament at her wrist shone through his dark curls, while she smoothed the hair upon his temples, idly but gently. In truth, the boy amused her, and she smiled upon him.

A shadow came between them and the sunlight. With a cry of terror Gentile fled, unregarded. For Maestro Ambrogio went directly to his wife, and took her hand.

"Come!" he said gravely, in a tone of pity rather than of remonstrance. " Come with me!"

She made no effort to resist him; and with a firm step he led her out into the garden. While they crossed it, all the sunshine seemed to come from her. She caught its glory like a mirror, and gave it back in playful gleams; then took it all away in one last radiant smile, when they passed into the laboratory and the door shut behind them. She had outdone the flowers; they looked cold and colorless. The perfect moment of the day had passed. The hours now could only droop and die.

What stillness in the house! The mute, unbidden guest, misfortune, had chosen it for his abode. Modesta barred the great door, and when the painter came she met him at the wicket, to put him off until the morrow with poor excuses. He entreated, threatened her ineffectually. He begged at least to have his drawing, but she denied him even that; she dared not tell him it had been destroyed. One word answered everything. To-morrow he should see her master; all would explain itself, all come right to-morrow. And while he protested, she closed the loop-hole in his face.

He went away and did not come again. There was no further disturbance from without; even the distant rumors of the city sunk to rest. The great blue silence overhead deepened and faded sombrely into the chilling pallor of the stars. Below, in the garden, the fireflies glanced about, the crickets droned, — no other sound broke in upon the quiet of the night; no sign of life, no movement from the workshop; there too all was black and still.

Bolt upright in her chair, hour by hour, Modesta sat and told her beads. From intervals of uneasy slumber in which she heard her master's voice calling her, she started up to listen breathlessly, to drop back and pray herself to sleep again. At last she felt sure that she had not been dreaming. " Modesta! Modesta!" the cry of distress came sharply and clearly, bringing her to her feet with an answering cry. But now the cool, gray tint of morning met her eyes. The drowsy notes of night were hushed. She could hear the twitter of the waking swallows, but nothing else.

She went to the laboratory door, and knocked repeatedly, then tried the latch; it yielded, and she stood for the first time on that forbidden ground.

The place was like some dream of a disordered mind. Piles of mouldy books; loose parchment leaves, yellow and illegible; flasks of metal, incrusted and corroded into fantastic shapes and colors; swollen monsters of glass with slender necks, emitting dull phosphoric light, or bearing old stains of substances long since distilled; mortars, and heaps of pounded drugs; fossils and charts, and livid specimens in bottles, — these things and more were huddled together in motley groups, or flung aside neglected. And in the midst of all, by the door of the furnace, which was choked with dying embers, crouched Maestro Ambrogio.

He seemed to have dropped asleep with his hand upon the bellows; they had fallen close beside him. The air of the room was full of dust, through which Modesta made her way with timid steps, hesitating to disturb her master, shrinking from the surrounding objects, yet eager to examine them. She stopped half stifled, drew back for freer breath, returned, went on. She could see more clearly now. Maestro Ambrogio was alone. Where then was her mistress? What had he done with her? At the form into which the question shaped itself Modesta stood still, trembling.

Here, close by, was the carved chest which had aroused her curiosity long ago. At that moment, through the little window to which she had climbed in former days, the first sunbeams slanted down. She saw at her feet a stone tablet, rudely inscribed with records of a dead people. She remembered others like it, unearthed among her own mountains ; and on the lid of the coffer at her side, she saw a sculptured figure, in high relief, perfect in form and feature, — the graven image of the stranger who had brought ill luck upon the house, the woman with the pagan name.

There she lay asleep, as Modesta had first seen her, with the clinging garment, the veil about her head, the ornament at her wrist; and her lips had the same enchanting smile upon them, — it was hard to believe that they were cut in alabaster. This seemed to be a living statue of one who in life had only seemed to live.

What did the chest hold ? Modesta must know that ; now was the very time. She tugged at the lid with all her might, but could not raise it. Slowly, without noise she pushed and pushed again, sliding it aside. Ashes there, and nothing else, — ashes, fine as dust ; stay, something more, on which the sun's rays glittered. It was the twisted thread of gold that Maestro Ambrogio's wife had worn.

With a cry Modesta staggered back; then, to save herself, caught at the alabaster cover which toppled and fell, dashed into a thousand pieces. Dust and ashes mingling made a thicker cloud. Life woke in the room. Mice scampered across it, squeaking ; spiders fled to hide themselves ; a bat flew wildly in and out of the dark corners. The embers of the furnace rattled down, and flickered into flame ; while poor Modesta waited with downcast eyes for her master's angry word. It did not come, and she looked up. The firelight flashed upon his face. It was a death-mask. The days of his reproof were over. All the vexations of the world were done for him.

Modesta returned to her native hills of the Mugello, and for many winters more her master's dead face haunted her, as the look he could never catch haunted the great painter all his life. It was a life of wandering, and he died in France years afterward. The picture he longed to make was never finished; but between him and every woman's face he painted came that mysterious remembrance, which, in spite of himself, his brush recorded. The world saw it, named it, handed down the name; and to this day, we know it as the smile of Leonardo.

THROUGH THE GATE OF DREAMS.

ON the longest day in one of these later years whose wine is not yet old enough to drink, whose history is still too recent to record, the ancient town of Mayence lay asleep in that radiant sunshine which, perhaps even more than its former commercial prosperity, may have given it the name of "golden." The wide Gutenberg-Platz was a blinding desert, with no shelter anywhere for man or beast; and Thorwaldsen's statue of the good printer looked parched and dry as the dusty laurel-wreath bound about his head at the last anniversary ceremonial and still clinging there. The white walls of the theatre turned toward him vast posters, in the type of his invention, hopelessly out of date. Its doors were closed indefinitely. Even the Café de Paris was silent and empty, but for its attendants and their presiding divinity, enshrined at her high desk and dozing behind her fan. The noonday glare had laid upon the place a potent spell which only far-reaching shadows could remove.

Just beyond the theatre, however, in the little

square of the Triton, it is always possible to draw a breath. There the boughs of the clipped lindens cast perpetual shade, with at least a look of refreshment in it. The fountain spouts and splashes and flings its foam-wreath down among the flowers, that thrive and blossom in colors which elsewhere would be uncomfortably bright. Midsummer in its fiercest mood can only salute that merry water-god with lowered lance, and leave him master of the field. So the townsman smiles upon him gratefully in a leisure moment, and drinks deep to him at some *Brauerei*, in draughts that have their foam-wreaths too. And the stranger with time at his command lingers on to eye the water wistfully; while the *Kellner* forgets to be alert, but leans against the door-post, limp, expressionless; and mine host fills his pipe, with a sigh of regret for the busy winter, as he wonders how long he has been reading his newspaper of yesterday upside down.

The only consumer of beer to be seen in the Triton-Platz on this particular afternoon was a pallid youth, whose looks, to put the adverse judgment mildly, told but little in his favor. His yellow hair, tangled and neglected, had grown much too long. His beard, also untrimmed, served no ornamental purpose, and was so thin and colorless that it did not even conceal the extreme plainness of his features. His broad-brimmed hat of soft felt and his long coat, unfashionably cut, had once

been dyed black, but were now threadbare. He
looked unkempt, uncouth, and rusty, even to the
worn-out clumsy shoes ; and the spectacles, through
which his watery blue eyes gained all their reflections of the universe, gave his face the blank, forbidding cast of an owl's in the daytime. The brain
behind it might well be a treasure-house of learn-
ing, but the medium of defence was apparently so
dull and impenetrable that no chance observer
would have cared to make an attack upon it. A
blue cotton umbrella and a shabby knapsack, hollow
in its folds, completed the accoutrements of this
odd soldier of fortune, who, whether sage or pedant,
had nothing of the personal charm that means
more than half the battle for such empty honors
as the world can give.

But within us all lurks that unknown quantity
the world cannot gauge, whose exact dimensions
remain a mystery even to ourselves. And this
shy, negative personage, distinguished solely by his
name of Einhard Becker, could display, in critical
moments, a trembling resolution akin to heroism,
— like that of the fighting unit who longs to run
away, but whose spirit keeps his face to the music.
The poor student — for such at least he surely was
— had faced his music more than once to find it
singularly discordant. And now again, his spirit
was sorely tried.

He was a native of Frankfort-on-the-Main, — the
old free town of which Heine has left a fond

remembrance in the saddest poem of all that his sad song-book holds : —

> " Frankfurt, du hegst viel Narrn und Bösewichter,
> Doch lieb' ich dich, du gabst dem deutschen Land
> Manch guten Kaiser und den besten Dichter,
> Und bist die Stadt wo ich die Holde fand."

" Many good emperors," of whom the first was Charlemagne. But if any drop of imperial blood diffused itself in Einhard Becker's veins, he was unaware of it. Though he had lost his parents so early in life that he could hardly be said to have known them, he did not lack abundant proof of his humble origin. A crabbed old uncle, Jacob Koberstein the saddler, had taken possession of the orphan boy, rearing him as his apprentice, with a certain rough fidelity. According to this high authority the elder Becker had been a good-for-nothing, whom the mother, Koberstein's sister, had persisted in marrying out of pure caprice. She had been told often enough that no good would come of such a marriage ; well, no good had come of it, as any one could see with half an eye. The case was always closed by this emphatic statement, which a significant glance at Einhard made doubly impressive ; and the boy would then be told to put up the shutters carefully, and to remember that his uncle was one of the best and thriftiest men in Frankfort. Einhard believed, of course, what was repeated in the same straightforward terms on almost every day of his life ; yet for some ancestral

sin he had been cursed with a soul above leather ;
and as he grew up, he became more and more
dreamy and unpractical, living in a world of his
own creation, far removed from the bustling, trade-
haunted *Zeil* of his daily walks, and evolved from
the text of all the books that came in his way.
Near his uncle's shop, a dealer in antiquities had a
cellar stored with musty volumes, which the boy
was allowed to turn over in his spare moments ;
sometimes too he obtained permission to carry
them home for stealthy reading in the watches of
the night by the flame of a candle-end. The anti-
quarian had a charitable heart, and taking pity
upon Einhard's hunger for mental improvement,
trusted him in this manner even with his rarest
treasures, entirely confident that his trust would
never be betrayed. For Einhard had, from the
first, shown something more than the scholar's
reverence, and he dealt with each leaf as tenderly
as though it were composed of golden tissue. Its
lines to him were lines of light, shining out upon him
from the sunny realms of poetry and romance. He
slept to walk hand in hand with gods and heroes ;
and even the trials of the day he learned to endure
patiently for the sake of what the night would bring.

His uncle Koberstein had one child, a daughter,
who seemed to Einhard's boyish fancy the embodiment of all that was good and beautiful. In point
of fact his cousin Minna's black eyes and rosy
cheeks, in all their freshness of youth, were suffi-

ciently prepossessing; but she had a high temper and a will of her own, and was a thorough Koberstein, the neighbors said, in a tone which implied something the reverse of complimentary. To Einhard, however, she always tried to appear at her best. Her way was his way, in the first place; then he amused her too. Behind the house there was a scrap of garden, where they would sometimes sit in the twilight, while he told her tales out of his wonderful books, to which she listened graciously. Once he made a story of his own, and told her that; and she thought it better than all the others. How could he help liking her? Once again, in his talk, he busied himself all the while with the cutting of their initials, interlaced, on the bench between them. Then she called for the knife, and hacked away at the wood unmercifully, obliterating the letters. It is to be feared that he liked her all the more for that. Who can tell?

Years went by. The city flourished as its trade increased; the sun of prosperity shone upon the house of Koberstein. A third pair of hands was needed there, and young Moritz Lahn, the butcher's son, entered upon his term of service. The new apprentice, though Einhard's junior by a year or two, was a stout, active lad, with a keen eye for his own advancement, and with little heart and less conscience. He lost no time in worming himself into old Jacob's good graces, and as it pleased Minna likewise to smile upon him, he was soon firmly established in the post of household favorite. It followed, as the night the day, that Einhard lost ground steadily. The poor relation became little better than the family drudge. Nothing he could do was exactly right; he was misjudged and slighted upon all occasions. Worse than that, his cousin played him false most cruelly by repeating some of his marvellous tales to Moritz, for whose companionship she now showed a decided preference; and the butcher's boy, displaying a savage dexterity that was perhaps inherited, turned the knife in Einhard's wound with many a mocking jest upon the subject of these confidences. The house of Koberstein was a small world, and the weakest went to the wall in it.

But for his good friends, the books, poor Einhard might have been driven to some desperate deed. As it was, he only imitated the tortoise, who shrinks into his shell to escape his tormentor. He made few complaints, spoke fewer and fewer words of any kind as the days went on. His brain was busy none the less. Stimulated always at night by the noble thoughts of others, his own thoughts came thick and fast, clamoring for expression. He trusted no one with them now; he did not even dare to write them down, but only committed them to memory in the form of verse, since verse was easier to remember. Often, though he did not know it, these were mere echoes of some master-mind, over which he had been brooding.

Even to utter a cry of the heart, at first, one's voice unconsciously repeats another's cry. But Einhard now and then could strike a note that was all his, and that would have rung out loud and clear with an echo of its own had there been any one to hear it.

So matters stood, with no change that was not for the worse, when Einhard was seventeen, and it happened that old Jacob Koberstein, going to bed late or getting up early, saw a gleam of light under the door of the garret where the boy slept alone. Bursting into the room without warning, he found Einhard wide awake, and hovering over a candle with a little vellum-bound book in his hand. Rage made him speechless for an instant; then he blew out the light, and telling his nephew to go to bed in the dark then and there and from that time forth, he departed, carrying off the book in spite of all that Einhard could say or do. It was a rare volume, belonging, of course, to the friendly dealer; and white with fear at the thought of its possible destruction, the boy crept down the stairs behind his uncle, who, however, did nothing more terrible than to lock it up in a certain iron-bound strong-box, of which he always carried the key. Thus relieved for the time Einhard went back to his room, and spent the rest of the night in devising means to get the priceless treasure safe into his hands again. He dared not betray its owner, lest this should be to cut off the source of his supplies.

15

His uncle's wrath would surely turn against the dealer, who would obtain the property only upon condition that the hideous crime of lending it should never be repeated. No; that would not do. He must keep his own counsel, await his opportunity, open the chest himself, when the favorable moment should occur. It would be but a moment, if he only had the key.

The key! How to get it? He had never before kept a book so long. Days passed in which he lived in dread of a demand for it; in which too his misery was aggravated by his uncle's persistent harshness. This had now taken an aggressive turn, not due, as Einhard believed, to the mere discovery of his midnight studies, but to quite a different cause. For some time old Jacob had missed various small sums of money, and in his own mind he secretly accused his unlucky nephew of pilfering them. The suspicion, for proof of which he kept sharp watch, changing his dislike to hatred, led him into acts of positive brutality. Einhard bore these new trials without complaint, as he had borne the others, still absorbed in his books, or rather, now, in one book which was no longer his.

Chance favored him. One stormy winter's night he was left alone with his uncle in their gloomy workshop. The room, littered now with piles of leather, and lighted by a flickering lamp, had been a kitchen in some former time. In one corner was a cavernous chimney, over which the wind howled dismally, bringing down stray drops of rain that pattered upon the hearth-stone. Moritz had taken himself off, but Einhard, grimy with dust and oil, still crouched at his bench ; while his uncle, bustling about, first put his work in order for the night, then drew a stool into the chimney-corner, and after kindling a fire, sat down by it to smoke his pipe in sullen silence. Einhard worked on mechanically, staying his hand now and then at a startling gust of the storm. Suddenly his eyes brightened ; he drew himself up ; his whole demeanor changed ; on the table, under the lamp, he had seen his uncle's keys. And in another moment, old Jacob's head drooped forward upon his breast, his right hand, with the pipe in it, dropped gently to his knee. He was sound asleep ; Einhard's hour had come.

In a flash the boy took off his shoes, crept to the table, caught up lamp and keys, and with every possible precaution made his way into the outer shop where the strong-box stood behind the little counter on the floor against the wall. He knelt beside it, trying each key in its turn until he found the right one. The lock yielded, the lid opened noiselessly ; under it he saw papers and bags of money, an odd trinket or two, a golden chain. He fumbled right and left to no purpose ; then scattered the things about until he came at last to the precious book, which he slipped at once into his pocket. The other contents he proceeded to put back with trembling care. In spite of all he could do, the papers rustled, the money clinked a little, — only a very little, but it was enough. There came a heavy step, a cry of rage; his shoulder was clutched by a strong, rough hand. Blindly he flung up his own which held one of the money bags, and struck his uncle full in the face. With an oath old Jacob fell in a heap, overturning the lamp, and floundering on the floor.

" Thief! thief!" he shouted.

"It is a lie!" cried Einhard, as he flung down the bag with all his might. It burst open, and the coins rolled right and left, glistening through the firelight of the inner room. Then, while the man wavered, in doubt which to pursue first, his treasure or his prey, the boy rushed to the door and fled out of it into the storm.

He was not followed. He turned one corner, then another; he heard no outcry, and could breathe freely. He was drenched, already numb with cold; but that mattered little since he had saved the book, which he now returned to the owner, telling him the story and begging shelter for the night. The dealer gave more than he asked, not only warming, feeding, and clothing him, but also offering to make his peace with Koberstein, if such a thing were possible. To this, however, Einhard would not listen.

" What then?" inquired his friend, who was a

timid, gentle soul, bowed with the weight of years. "What in the world is to become of you?"

"Anything in the world but that," replied the boy, stoutly. "To-morrow I will tell you."

So he went to bed, and tossed for awhile restlessly. Then he fell into a sleep disturbed by dreams, made up, as dreams often are, from shreds of actual experience stretched and twisted by a wilful fancy. One of these was strangely vivid. He saw a city square, long unfamiliar, that he had seen, indeed, but once, as a child in his father's arms. His father held him now, showing him the trees and flowers; there were little tables too, and he heard the sound of running water. Then his father was gone, and he stood erect, a grown man, facing an angry crowd that threatened him. By his side in the dress of another age knelt a fantastic figure, old, feeble, and deformed, imploring help.

"The world!" the stranger whispered. "It is all against you. Fight it, conquer it, or it will tear us limb from limb."

There came a struggle; the crowd seemed to sweep over him and bear him down. All passed, leaving him in cool, deep silence, lying alone under the trees, with his face to the stars, through which faint flushes of the dawn came stealing up. And then he woke to find it all a dream, except the morning light that shone around him, thrice clear and serene in contrast to his night of storms.

"Mayence!" he murmured; "it was Mayence! And it is there that I must go."

He remembered that in this neighboring city lived his father's cousin, whom, to be sure, he had never seen. But the man was by trade a printer, and must therefore have a certain sympathy with books. That he was wretchedly poor there could be little doubt; yet this thought only strengthened Einhard in his resolve, for he knew instinctively that the poor always greet poverty with a gentleness which is often wanting in the rich man's treatment of it. Whatever might result, his appeal for advice and help, but not for charity, would at least be kindly heard. To Mayence, then, to Mayence! the moment that another night should shield him from his uncle's eyes. His old friend, who would have reconciled him to the saddler, made fruitless objections; then urged upon him money for the journey, which Einhard proudly declined. He had money of his own, he said. The dealer had turned the boy's pockets inside out, and knew that they contained only a few copper coins. But he accepted the statement gravely, contenting himself with such comfortable gifts of clothing as could be forced upon his guest, whose departure, under cover of the darkness, he was already speeding when the door opened and Minna Koberstein presented herself.

Einhard drew back in dismay; his imagination already pictured the dungeon to which he would be dragged forthwith, now that his hiding-place was known. But Minna had only guessed at it, and had shrewdly kept her own counsel. Out of her cousin's slender store of worldly goods she had filled a knapsack with the things most needful for a journey, since he must go away. Her father was very violent; it would not do to venture into his sight. Did Einhard know of his dreadful charges, which she knew were false? His uncle could not be convinced of their injustice; but she pledged herself to bring him to reason in Einhard's absence. Yes; he must go away, for a time.

"For all time!" said Einhard to himself. Then, touched by Minna's impulsive kindness, he described in detail his adventure, and accepted gratefully her friendly offices. She had won her old place in his heart again; it was with tears in his eyes that he bade her farewell. So the three parted upon the threshold, and went their several ways. She to her present care of turning old Jacob's wit the seamy side within; the dealer to his mouldy records of the past; and Einhard straight out to meet the future, and make it stand and deliver whatever good fortune it should bring.

He slept that night by the roadside, with his knapsack for a pillow. All day he followed the dusty highway, procuring a scanty meal under the porch of some village inn, and then trudging on with a light heart so long as his money lasted;

but it was all gone by the next noon, when, drawing near the gates of a town, tired, hungry, and
despondent, he stopped to rest and take thought of
the morrow.   Rather than beg he opened his pack
in search of something to offer in exchange for
food, and immediately out dropped a roll of money,
— enough to supply his moderate wants for days
and weeks.   Who but Minna could have done this?
He blessed her for it a thousand times.   How
bright the skies were now; how yellow were the
cornfields that he passed, how green the vineyards!
But his harvest lay beyond, under the spires of
Mayence; already against the clear sky they twinkled, with all their vanes, like beckoning fingers.
The sun set, and these same towers grew gray and
cold as he approached them.   Then the chimes
rang out, muffled and mellowed by the distance, —
a low breathing of unseen bells rather than their
uplifted voices.   " Fortune! fortune! " he half
heard them say, as if the note of promise were
meant only for his ears.   At the sound his heart
beat higher, though the twilight deepened, until at
last he came to the broad river and the mighty
bridge, over which he strode with quickened pace,
out of the darkness of solitude into flaring streets
filled with the darker indifference of unknown
faces.

    Since the day he was driven forth from Eden,
man's state has been little better than that of the
pack-horse, never free of his burden, but merely

exchanging one load for another in all his wanderings through the world. At the first glance Einhard's share of the weight would seem to have become no lighter under the printer's apprenticeship upon which he entered. But actually, both in body and in mind, he was much relieved. His new-found relative received him with kindness, made room for him at his own table, obtained for him this employment, which, drudgery as it was, brought with it enormous compensations. If to handle type afforded him no special joy, there were manuscripts that he could decipher, printed pages from which something could be learned in a furtive glance, the glow of excitement that a good line gives to one who can use his brains. Furthermore, in hours of freedom he found opportunity secretly to set up lines and pages of his own with which his mind had long been teeming. And though his great thoughts dwindled when he met them in this manner, face to face, at least they were neither hasty nor ill-considered; it was like seeing his own heart in a mirror to read them. So, hoping always to do better, and growing with his work, he went on, slowly adding leaf after leaf to a book of his own making in all senses of the word.

Once established in his new calling he made it his first care to thank his cousin for the mysterious gift discovered in his knapsack at a desperate moment. He wrote that he had spent but little of the money; that he only waited to make good the sum out of his earnings before restoring it in full. For a long time this letter was left unanswered, and the answer, when it came, was singularly cold. Minna disclaimed all knowledge of the money; she had given him none. She wished her cousin well, but she held out no hope of a change in her father's views concerning him. Obviously old Jacob still believed his nephew to be a thief. Did Minna think so too? Was her coldness due to that? Or was it merely that she cared a little less for Einhard than for his former rival, Moritz Lahn?

Who, then, could have concealed the roll of bank-notes in his wallet? Who but the first cause of all his joys and troubles, the kind old treasure-seeker whose offers of money he had proudly rejected? To him, therefore, Einhard addressed a letter, which returned long afterward with the seal unbroken. The good dealer in imprints had scanned his last title-page, and had gone the musty way of all documents, however guarded. He was dead as the Sibyl's books; and limited as were his friendships, Einhard counted one friend less in the world.

He laid the sum by, and living frugally, increased it little by little. He dreaded beggary even more than death itself, and this wholesome terror spared him many an after pang; for there came a dull year when he, in common with many others, fell out of employment. And it was to Einhard, the youngest of them all, that some of these despairing

people applied for temporary help, which he gener-
ously accorded so far as possible. This disaster
became also the spur to his intent, driving him
suddenly forward into the world of letters. With
fear and trembling he offered to a publisher his
small foundling of literature, which was received
and adopted, admired even. It actually brought
him money, — a pittance, it is true, but still, money.
He lost no time in setting to work upon another
which had long been seething in his brain. This
should clinch his first hold upon success, make
him something more than a minor poet, — perhaps
a great one. If he could only finish it! But he
was miserably poor, and haunted by a thousand
nervous fancies. One day his work seemed absolutely worthless; the next, it hung fire altogether;
still another, he was all a-glow with it, but there
stood starvation knocking at the door, eager to run
a race with his pen. Fortunately there set in an
early spring, — that season of hope to all, and
especially to the poor man, for it puts money in his
purse, with a promise of long exemption from the
need of light and fuel. For his sake would it were
always scorching midsummer in all climes the sun
shines on; how much less pitiable are the poor of
the tropics than the poor of London.

And now we have followed the small circle back
to the very point of our departure, coming once
more upon Einhard Becker seated in the Triton-
Platz of Mayence, absorbed in a new problem very

difficult to solve. His cousin Minna had written to him again, and this time of her own accord. The evil spirit of the house of Koberstein had been exorcised at last. Moritz Lahn, now expelled ignominiously, was proved to be the real culprit for whose crime the innocent had suffered. Her good father, she wrote, longed to make all the amends in his power. Through her he recalled Einhard upon the most flattering of terms, — not as an apprentice, but as a master. They would share and share alike; henceforth he should be treated as old Jacob's son, — as his successor; and Minna, imploring him to come back, threw, it seemed, more than a sister's love into the scale. But all this depended upon one condition. Einhard must pledge himself to give up his books, and fix all his thoughts on leather. There must be no poetry in his life, unless her love, that had waxed and waned capriciously, could be accounted a poetic thing.

Upon receiving this letter, in one of his exultant moods, Einhard was inclined to laugh at it. Inured as he was to poverty, what were its hardships compared with his uncle's tyranny, of which there still remained the vivid recollection? What were the definite material comforts that could outweigh his illimitable hopes of fame? He took up his pen to set aside temptation with a single stroke. But he was not quick enough; before it touched the paper doubts assailed him. He hesitated, dropped the pen, and read the letter once more. After all it promised much. Life-long immunity from care should not be considered lightly. And he had loved his cousin once. She had done her best at times to quench the boyish passion which now bade fair to revive under the destroyer's hand. Already he longed for a sight of her. Was not success in love the best that mortal man could hope to know? Yes; it was everything. To forego that joy for the delusive one of fame was like turning from a fire to snatch warmth from a star.

Lost now in a maze of deliberation, that day he wrote no word. All night he lay awake, and in the morning, springing up resolutely, he composed a line of acceptance, which he immediately destroyed; then he went out, and strolled aimlessly through the town, staring at the shops, noting how sleek and comfortable the tradesmen looked, until he came to a saddler's window, and drew back in disgust. The smell of the leather was enough to make him miserable. And so, tired and faint with the heat, he turned at last into the Triton-Platz, where, at that hour, he found much merriment and clinking of glasses. One by one the other citizens withdrew to their affairs. Einhard was left alone long before his simple meal was finished. That did not trouble him, however. He knew the square well, and loved it from the tenderest associations. It was just there, across the way, that his father had held him up to look at the fountain years ago. The cool solitude of the place was very grateful to

him ; he would stay on here until he had settled his
burning question once for all.   He spread Minna's
letter out before him, and calling for pen and
paper, prepared again to answer it; but he got no
farther than the scribbling of his name.   As he sat
with knit brows, forgetful of his looks, the picture
of helpless indecision, the waiters smiled a little,
then yawned and dozed, leaving him to himself.
Like all waiters, they knew their world, and were
not to be moved by any trifling eccentricity in it.

The shadows grew longer and sharper ; the day
was drawing to a close; the square roused itself
and gave signs of life.   Two young men placed
themselves at a table near that at which Einhard
still sat scribbling his name abstractedly.   They
called for beer, and chattered over some gossip of
the town.   Their talk was interrupted by a noise
of distant shouting, which came nearer and nearer,
till there turned into the square a man's figure of
inconceivable oddity, followed by a troop of mocking boys, who, however, kept at a safe distance,
since now and then their victim paused to threaten
them.   He was withered and shrunken, covered
with dust from head to foot ; strange garments
hung about him loosely, but these were of a faded
splendor, rich in their material.   As he approached
with shambling and uncertain gait he looked like
some mask that had lost his way in a bygone car-
nival, and had been wandering about the earth
ever since, vainly trying to find it.   Coming up to

the café-door he peered timidly at Einhard's neighbors with eyes that seemed to fear the light, and
then asked them to tell him what day of the year
it was.

The men laughed, but made no other answer.
The boys, encouraged by the sympathy of these
new allies, looked about for stones to throw at the
bewildered stranger, who paid them no heed, but
addressing the older of the two men, put his hands
together with a quaint, imploring gesture, and
repeated his question.

"Tell me, sir, I pray you," he begged in a
cracked voice, "what is the date of the year?"

"How should I know?" retorted the man, with
a laugh. "There it is; read it yourself." And
he pointed as he spoke toward the theatre-wall, on
which clung the remnant of a play-bill, bearing a
date, it is true, but one long past.

The stranger bowed with a grateful word, then
moving slowly to the wall, shaded his eyes with
his hand, and looked up at the tattered poster.

Einhard sprung to his feet indignantly.

"Why did you tell him that?" he asked.

"Why not?" said the man. "Who the devil
are you?"

"I am neither a coward nor a liar," said Einhard,
in a passion, "and you are both."

With an inarticulate cry of rage the man flew at
Einhard's throat. There was a struggle, in which
the student had the better of it. They fell to the

ground together, Einhard uppermost; but his opponent's comrade interfered, and after him the waiters. Chairs and tables were overturned in a prolonged scuffle, from which Einhard suddenly found himself extricated, he knew not how, and leaning against the café-wall for breath. A shower of small stones rattled about his ears; while the poor dwarf, who had flown to him for protection, crouched at his feet and clasped his knees. Beside him the fray went on; others had joined in it; it threatened to become general. The uproar grew louder and wilder; already the square was filling up with a curious crowd. The boys danced with savage delight, like demons, and fired a second volley indiscriminately. One of the stones struck in the face the innocent cause of all the mischief, who moaned piteously.

"The world!" he cried in a voice faint with terror. "It is always so in the world. Help, good master! Save me!"

Einhard caught up a chair to attack one of the troop now venturing within reach; but at that moment the window behind him opened, a hand grasped his arm and dragged him in, together with the strange companion, who had fastened upon him like a crab.

"Be off with you!" said the host, for it was he. "Do you want to bring the house about our ears?"

And he pushed them toward a small door at the back of the café leading to a narrow, quiet street, already dark in the deepening twilight. The dwarf now took the lead, and as though he knew his way perfectly, hurried Einhard along, by one turn after another, until they came out into the open Schiller-Platz, near the outskirts of the town, where all was cool and still. Its old lime-trees flung about them fantastic shadows, in which their own were lost, as they went on to a noiseless fountain hidden away among the leaves. Here his guide stopped to refresh himself by dipping his hands and face into the basin; and Einhard, finding that he too was bruised and bleeding, did the same.

The fountain is surmounted by a granite pillar, said to be a relic of Charlemagne's palace at Ingelheim, and certainly so old that this statement of its origin has never been disputed. As Einhard Becker lifted his face from the refreshing water he saw that the dwarf had left his side and had climbed to the base of the column, where he knelt for a moment to lay his lips upon the stone, reverently. Then, with an adroitness of which he had appeared before incapable, he swung himself quietly to the earth again, and drawing nearer, plucked Einhard gently by the sleeve. His eyes had lost their dulness, and were keen and piercing. His whole expression too had changed, as if he had gathered strength and courage from the darkness, like a nocturnal animal. Einhard looked at him in wonder, waiting for him to speak. At that moment the cathedral clock struck the hour, and the

16

stranger laid his finger on his lips, counting inaudibly the strokes of the bell, and listening for its last vibration to die away.

" Nine ! " he muttered. " So late, and they told me nothing. But you are not like the others," he added, turning to Einhard confidently. " I can trust you."

" Fully," said Einhard. " What help do you need ? " Strange as this presence was, he did not shrink from it ; rather it drew him closer by some bond of sympathy wholly unaccountable. Then, in a voice clear and resonant as the cathedral-bell itself, the man put his singular question for the third time, —

" Tell me, I pray you, what is the date of the year ? "

" Midsummer-day," said Einhard, smiling at his insistence, and puzzled by the reiteration of his trivial demand.

" But the year, — the year ? "

Einhard gave this information also ; the other repeating the words thoughtfully, and then expressing his thanks with grateful earnestness.

" You have done me double service ; you took my part, — you saved me from those lying curs. Yet by your looks I see that you are most unhappy. They have tormented you too, down there in the world."

" No," said Einhard, sighing ; for Minna's letter, still unanswered, lay like a leaden weight upon his heart. "I am my own tormentor. I long to soar, and dare not trust my wings."

"A poor confession!" said the dwarf, in a tone almost savage in its sternness. "Is the penance you call life so precious that you cannot risk the loss of it, even for the stars?"

"Dead worlds!" replied Einhard, mournfully. "They mock us with a beauty unattainable. Look up! Between us and them lies all the blackness of oblivion."

"Yes," was the bitter answer; "it is a fine thing to deal in leather."

Einhard started. "What do you mean?" demanded he.

"O poet!" said the warning voice, softened now into a note of sadness; "the price they ask you is too dear for happiness so brief. Let the earth go, and listen to the soul that pleads in you for an immortal life. Win that, or fail only in striving to attain it. Come with me, and I will show you what it is to live."

"Where would you have me go?"

The dwarf pointed toward one of the city gates, rising between them and the western stars. "To my master, who is waiting there for my return."

"Beyond the gate?"

"Ay, truly. Beyond the gate, — beyond the gate of dreams; into the grandeur of the past, the splendor of an unknown future, where no man living has been before you."

" You promise much," said Einhard, with a smile. " But can you make the grandeur and the splendor last ? Will not the poor dreamer, when he wakes, be all the poorer for his dreams ?"

" Have faith," the dwarf replied. " I make the unreal real. When you have passed my master's threshold you will never wake. To you, hereafter, life will be the dream."

" What more can I ask ? " said Einhard, confidently, " except that you shall keep your word. Farewell, house of Koberstein ! " As he spoke his hand closed upon the letter, and with it he lifted from his heart its intolerable load. He flung the crumpled paper into the fountain with a sigh of relief. " I will go," said he.

" Follow me, then," returned the dwarf, as he drew his tattered cloak about him. " This way, — through the shadows."

Hugging the darkness, so far as it was possible, they went on in silence to a flight of stone steps that led them to a terrace high above the city. At this commanding point, while the guide stopped for breath, Einhard turned to look down upon the spires and housetops, the frowning roof of the cathedral, the wide sweep of the Rhine and its sentinel peaks of the Niederwald in all their varying degrees of blackness. A murmur rose from the pavement where countless lamps traced out the streets and squares like strings of jewels ; and one shrill voice shot up to them, cutting the air, as though borne on the feathered shaft of an arrow. But it did not come from the Triton-Platz; there all was peace itself under the overarching leaves.

They followed the terrace to the city wall, and beyond it, through the Binger Gate, into the open country. Here the dwarf, quickening his pace, strode out along the smooth turnpike that stretched away immeasurably.

" Is not this the road to Zahlbach ?" asked Einhard, breaking at last their oppressive silence.

" No; to Ingelheim," replied the other, without stopping even to turn his head. Time pressed with him, since they had far to go.

" To Ingelheim," repeated Einhard, under his breath. The word recalled old legends of his earliest friends, the books, and made him regard the distorted figure trudging on before him with something more than reverence, yet with no thought of fear. Who was his master ? To what threshold were they tending ? The question of the year, which he had asked so often, tallied perfectly with a tale the student knew by heart. If that tale were true, the mysterious messenger could work him only good. To pass that noble master's portal, and make all after-life one glorious rec-ollection, would be, in truth, to enter through the gate of dreams.

They were on high land now; the night wind blew fresh and cool. Dark vineyards opened out before them to the darker Rhine shore, already

miles away. The road kept its due westward
course, rising gradually, and bringing them nearer
to the stars, — so near that myriads came out where
none had been before. A great meteor swept
slowly across the sky in a trail of light; a hare
fled from them into the thicket; a night-bird flew
over, uttering a dismal cry   But they met no
human creature, and the dwarf, holding his even
gait, left all these sights and sounds unheeded.

They had walked thus for more than two hours,
when the road began gradually to descend toward
the village of Ingelheim, which lay asleep under
its shadowy roof-lines ; but on one side of the
way the land still rose in an abrupt slope, unbroken and unwooded. There the guide suddenly
stopped, to make sure that he was observed ; then,
beckoning Einhard to follow, he plunged into the
long grass, and proceeded to climb the hill. The
crickets vaulted before him as he passed, the rank
weeds and field-flowers he had brushed aside
sprung back drenching Einhard with dew. So
they climbed on, up the height and over the brow
of it to a wide, wind-swept plateau that looked all
the more desolate for certain detached fragments
of a ruin rising massively against the sky. The
rough-hewn walls, mediæval in character, must
once have enclosed a dwelling of splendor and
solidity ; but roofs and towers and pinnacles lay
in the earth under huge mounds heaped over all
like graves of a colossal race, and it seemed as if

the crumbling arches that remained would long ago have fallen too, but for stout branches of ivy binding the stones together and sustaining them. All broken lines had been softened and beautified by its glossy mantle, glistening now at every fold in the light of the one-eyed, waning moon that rose above this memorial of a vanished age as the intruders drew near. Then Einhard whispered, while his companion paused for breath once more : " It is the hill of Charlemagne."

" Hark ! " returned the dwarf, with a warning gesture ; and from some distant point within the ruins came the sound of a horn, in low, sweet notes, faintly blowing. The dwarf advanced, drew himself up, and answered the signal with a wild, unearthly cry that echoed and re-echoed through the empty arches. In a moment the unseen warder blew his horn again, and then all was silent except the rustling of the leaves.

With swift, noiseless steps the messenger returned to Einhard's side.

" Give me your hand," he whispered, " we will go in together. Hush ! not a word ! Only when I give the sign speak without fear ; until then silence."

So, hand in hand and silently, they passed slowly on over black bars of shadow, through grass-grown courts, roofless and deserted, — now following some line of ruined wall to climb it at a favorable point where the matted ivy secured their foothold, and

the knights, with one voice. A hundred swords flashed from their sheaths. All were alert and ready; yet no light came into their faces; they still slept, moved only by the impulse of a dream.

The king alone woke to life. His eyes opened; he rose in his place and looked about him. On the instant all was still again. Then he spoke, in tones that made the arches ring.

"Messenger from without the gate, what is the date of the year?"

Einhard looked at the dwarf, who made no reply, but gave instead their preconcerted signal; and the student, comprehending it, rose in his turn, and advancing to the royal dais knelt at the emperor's feet and answered him.

His noble face grew clouded, and he sighed heavily as he addressed once more the throng below him.

"Back, comrades! The hour is not come."

The swords rattled down into their scabbards, and with a dull clang the armed men dropped, one and all, into repose. Murmurous echoes spread through the outer courts, swelling and subsiding, as if a wave of the sea had dashed itself to pieces. Then the stillness of desolation settled over all.

But the king bent upon his new-found messenger a keen, penetrating glance that seemed to search through Einhard's inmost soul. Gradually his face resumed its former calmness, and the smile returned to it.

"The hour will come," he said gently, "though it be long delayed. We, who reign forever, can read men's hearts in faces; and in the face and heart before me there are signs of promise."

"In mine?" said Einhard, trembling.

"Yes. The age of chivalry is past, but only for a season; and on the toilers we, who wait, depend. Not he alone is great who slaughters armies. To wrestle with the world, and conquer it; to have no thought that is not half divine; to give the thought a word that shall vibrate in all hearts, stirring them to noble deeds, and make the meanest slave a hero, — this is to be greater than a king. This done, the earth sweeps back into its golden age."

"Alas!" said Einhard, with a sigh, "what man can hope to hold a place in every heart?"

"None that will not strive for it. What! are there no mortals who have put on immortality?"

"Oh, pardon me!" replied the student, as he humbly bowed his head. "I speak to one of these."

With a gracious gesture the emperor motioned Einhard to a low seat beside him.

"Sit here by me," he said, "and tell me some story of the past. For I am restless with long years of waiting. Only labor can bring happiness. Be true, then, to gifts that Heaven has bestowed, and use them well, however men reward them or despise them. Work, work; and work again!

God grant that in the after ages unending toil may be both mine and thine!"

Then Einhard, half from memory and half in verses of his own that formed themselves without an effort, recited a legend of the day that survives eternally in the chronicle of Roland. Little by little, all the light of the hall went out, and the sleepers faded away, one by one, until only the watchful eyes of the dwarfs were left, glittering like glow-worms. And when the tale was finished the king sunk to sleep, with his arm upon the table, his cheek upon his hand. Einhard too slept soundly; and the memorable night passed on, as all nights must, however memorable, to become a mere remembrance of things that were, while the light of a new day stole into its place and slowly illumined half the world.

Einhard woke to find himself lying alone in the sunshine under the ruined entrance of the crumbling, ivied wall. He beat upon the door, but could not move it, and nothing moved within. He turned away sadly, lingering and looking back, inclining to believe that he had only dreamed. As he came into the open field a lark flew up in a joyous ecstasy of song, singing, singing, and still singing, with a full throat, — an invisible rapture of the blue distance. Then Einhard's look grew lighter, and his heart leaped as he went down toward the spires of Mayence.

"It was no dream," he murmured. "It was a

step toward the eternal goal. What need I care henceforth for pain or pleasure in this narrow world? The nobler life will come hereafter; and through one poor soul, at least, the appointed hour will not be delayed. Oh, emperor! I strive for immortality. Unending toil shall be both thine and mine!"

THE END.

BRIEF LIST OF BOOKS OF FICTION PUBLISHED BY CHARLES SCRIBNER'S SONS, 743-745 BROADWAY, NEW YORK.

Mary Adams.

AN HONORABLE SURRENDER. (16mo, $1.00.)

"The story belongs distinctly to the realistic school of modern fiction. The situations are those of every day. The characters are not in the least eccentric; the dialogue is never extravagant; the descriptive and analytical passages are neither obtrusive nor too prolix. The sum of all these negations is a charming book, full of a genuine human interest."—*The Portland Advertiser.*

William Waldorf Astor.

VALENTINO: An Historical Romance. (12mo, $1.00).—SFORZA: A Story of Milan. (12mo, $1.00.)

"The story is full of clear-cut little tableaux of mediæval Italian manners, customs, and observances. The movement throughout is spirited, the reproduction of bygone times realistic. Mr. Astor has written a romance which will heighten the reputation he made by 'Valentino.'"—*The New York Tribune.*

Arlo Bates.

A WHEEL OF FIRE. (12mo, paper, 50 cts.; cloth, $1.00.)

"The novel deals with character rather than incident, and is evolved from one of the most terrible of moral problems with a subtlety not unlike that of Hawthorne. One cannot enumerate all the fine points of artistic skill which make this study so wonderful in its insight, so rare in its combination of dramatic power and tenderness."—*The Critic.*

Hjalmar H. Boyesen.

FALCONBERG. Illustrated (12mo, $1.50)—GUNNAR. (Sq. 12mo, paper, 50 cts.; cloth, $1.25)—TALES FROM TWO HEMISPHERES. (Sq. 12mo, $1.00)—ILKA ON THE HILL TOP, and Other Stories. (Sq. 12mo, $1.00) —QUEEN TITANIA (Sq. 12mo, $1.00).

"Mr. Boyesen's stories possess a sweetness, a tenderness, and a drollery that are fascinating, and yet they are no more attractive than they are strong "—*The Home Journal.*

BRIEF LIST OF BOOKS OF FICTION PUBLISHED BY CHARLES SCRIBNER'S SONS, 743-745 BROADWAY, NEW YORK.

Mary Adams.

AN HONORABLE SURRENDER. (16mo, $1.00.)

"The story belongs distinctly to the realistic school of modern fiction. The situations are those of every day. The characters are not in the least eccentric; the dialogue is never extravagant; the descriptive and analytical passages are neither obtrusive nor too prolix. The sum of all these negations is a charming book, full of a genuine human interest."—*The Portland Advertiser.*

William Waldorf Astor.

VALENTINO: An Historical Romance. (12mo, $1.00).—**SFORZA: A Story of Milan.** (12mo, $1.00.)

"The story is full of clear-cut little tableaux of mediæval Italian manners, customs, and observances. The movement throughout is spirited, the reproduction of bygone times realistic. Mr. Astor has written a romance which will heighten the reputation he made by 'Valentino.'"—*The New York Tribune.*

Arlo Bates.

A WHEEL OF FIRE. (12mo, paper, 50 cts.; cloth, $1.00.)

"The novel deals with character rather than incident, and is evolved from one of the most terrible of moral problems with a subtlety not unlike that of Hawthorne. One cannot enumerate all the fine points of artistic skill which make this study so wonderful in its insight, so rare in its combination of dramatic power and tenderness."—*The Critic.*

Hjalmar H. Boyesen.

FALCONBERG. Illustrated (12mo, $1.50)—**GUNNAR.** (Sq. 12mo, paper, 50 cts.; cloth, $1.25)—**TALES FROM TWO HEMISPHERES.** (Sq. 12mo, $1.00)—**ILKA ON THE HILL TOP, and Other Stories.** (Sq. 12mo, $1.00)—**QUEEN TITANIA** (Sq. 12mo, $1.00).

"Mr. Boyesen's stories possess a sweetness, a tenderness, and a drollery that are fascinating, and yet they are no more attractive than they are strong"—*The Home Journal.*

H. C. Bunner.

THE STORY OF A NEW YORK HOUSE. Illustrated by A. B. Frost (12mo, $1.25)—**THE MIDGE.** (12mo, paper, 50 cts.; cloth, $1.00)—**IN PARTNER-SHIP.** With Brander Matthews (12mo, paper, 50 cts.; cloth, $1.00).

"It is Mr. Bunner's delicacy of touch and appreciation of what is literary art that give his writings distinctive quality. Everything Mr. Bunner paints shows the happy appreciation of an author who has not alone mental discernment, but the artistic appreciation. The author and the artist both supplement one another in this excellent 'Story of a New York House.' "—*The New York Times.*

Frances Hodgson Burnett.

THAT LASS O' LOWRIE'S. Illustrated (paper, 50 cents; cloth, $1.25)—**HAWORTH'S.** Illustrated (12mo, $1.25)—**THROUGH ONE ADMINISTRA-TION.** (12mo, $1.50)—**LOUISIANA.** (12mo, $1.25)—**A FAIR BARBARIAN.** (12mo, paper, 50 cts.; cloth, $1.25)—**VAGABONDIA.** A Love Story. (12mo, paper, 50 cts.; cloth, $1.25)—**SURLY TIM, and Other Stories** (12mo, $1.25).

The above 7 vols., in uniform cloth binding, $9.00 per set.

THE PRETTY SISTER OF JOSÉ. Illustrated by C. S. Reinhart (12mo, $1.00).

LITTLE LORD FAUNTLEROY. (Sq. 8vo, $2.00).—**SARAH CREWE; or, What Happened at Miss Minchin's.** (Sq. 8vo, $1.00).—**LITTLE SAINT ELIZABETH, and Other Stories.** (12mo, $1.50). Illustrated by R. B. Birch.

Earlier Stories by the same author, each 16mo, paper covers.

LINDSAY'S LUCK (30 cts.)—**PRETTY POLLY PEMBERTON** (40 cts.)—**KATHLEEN** (40 cts.)—**THEO** (30 cts.)—**MISS CRESPIGNY** (30 cts.).

"Mrs. Burnett discovers gracious secrets in rough and forbidding natures—the sweetness that often underlies their bitterness—the soul of goodness in things evil. She seems to have an intuitive perception of character. If we apprehend her personages, and I think we do clearly, it is not because she describes them to us, but because they reveal themselves in their actions. Mrs. Burnett's characters are as veritable as Thackeray's."—RICHARD HENRY STODDARD.

William Allen Butler.

DOMESTICUS. A Tale of the Imperial City (12mo, $1.25.).

"Under a veil made intentionally transparent, the author maintains a running fire of good-natured hits at contemporary social follies. There is a delicate love story running through the book. The author's style is highly finished. One might term it old-fashioned in its exquisite choiceness and precision."—*The New York Journal of Commerce.*

George W. Cable.

THE GRANDISSIMES, (12mo, $1.25)—**OLD CREOLE DAYS.** (12mo, cloth, $1.25; also in two parts, 16mo, cloth, each, 75 cts.; paper, each, 30 cts.)— **DR. SEVIER.** (12mo, paper, 50 cts.; cloth, $1.25)—**BONAVENTURE.** A Prose Pastoral of Acadian Louisiana (12mo, Paper, 50 cents; $1.25.)

The set, 4 vols., $5.00.

"There are few living American writers who can reproduce for us more perfectly than Mr. Cable does, in his best moments, the speech, the manners, the whole social atmosphere of a remote time and a peculiar people. A delicious flavor of humor penetrates his stories."—*The New York Tribune.*

Edward Eggleston.

ROXY. Illustrated (12mo, $1.50)—**THE CIRCUIT RIDER.** Illustrated (12mo, $1.50).

"Dr. Eggleston's fresh and vivid portraiture of a phase of life and manners, hitherto almost unrepresented in literature ; its boldly contrasted characters, and its unconventional, hearty, religious spirit, took hold of the public imagination."—*The Christian Union.*

Erckmann-Chatrian.

THE CONSCRIPT. Illustrated—**WATERLOO.** Illustrated (Sequel to The Conscript)—**MADAME THERESE—THE BLOCKADE OF PHALSBURG.** Illustrated—**THE INVASION OF FRANCE IN 1814.** Illustrated—**A MILLER'S STORY OF THE WAR.** Illustrated.

The National Novels, each $1.25 ; the set, 6 vols., $7.50.

FRIEND FRITZ. A Tale of the Banks of the Lauter (12mo, paper, 50 cts.; cloth, $1.25).

Harold Frederic.

SETH'S BROTHER'S WIFE. (12mo, $1.25).—**THE LAWTON GIRL.** (12mo, $1.25; Paper, 50 cents).

The story has a very strong, human, and pathetic side, and the trials, struggles, and accomplishments of "The Lawton Girl" are depicted with delicate sympathy and with admirable art.

Octave Thanet.

EXPIATION. Illustrated by A. B. Frost. (12mo, Paper, 50 cents; Cloth, $1.00.)

"This remarkable novel shows an extraordinary grasp of dramatic possibilities as well as an exquisite delicacy of character drawing. Miss French has with this work taken her place among the very foremost of American writers of fiction.—*Boston Beacon.*

James Anthony Froude.

THE TWO CHIEFS OF DUNBOY. An Irish Romance of the Last Century. (12mo, paper, 50 cts.; cloth, $1.50.)

"The narrative is full of vigor, spirit, and dramatic power. It will unquestionably be widely read, for it presents a vivid and life-like study of character with romantic color and adventurous incident for the background."— *The New York Tribune.*

Robert Grant.

FACE TO FACE. (12mo, paper, 50 cents; cloth, $1.25.)

"This is a well-told story, the interest of which turns upon a game of cross purposes between an accomplished English girl, posing as a free and easy American Daisy Miller, and an American gentleman, somewhat given to aping the manners of the English."— *The Buffalo Express.*

Edward Everett Hale.

PHILIP NOLAN'S FRIENDS. Illustrated (12mo, Paper, 50 cents; Cloth, $1.75.)

"There is no question, we think, that this is Mr. Hale's completest and best novel. The characters are for the most part well drawn, and several of them are admirable."— *The Atlantic Monthly.*

Marion Harland.

JUDITH: A Chronicle of Old Virginia. (12mo, paper, 50 cts.; cloth, $1 00) —HANDICAPPED. (12mo, $1.50).—WITH THE BEST INTENTIONS. A Midsummer Episode. (12mo, Cloth, $1.25; Paper, 50 cents.)

"Fiction has afforded no more charming glimpses of old Virginia life than are found in this delightful story, with its quaint pictures, its admirably drawn characters, its wit, and its frankness."— *The Brooklyn Daily Times.*

Joel Chandler Harris.

FREE JOE, and Other Georgian Sketches. (12mo, paper, 50 cts., cloth, $1.00.)

"The author's skill as a story writer has never been more felicitously illustrated than in this volume. The title story is meagre almost to baldness in incident, but its quaint humor, its simple but broadly outlined characters, and, above all, its touching pathos, combine to make it a masterpiece of its kind."— *The New York Sun.*

Augustus Allen Hayes.

THE JESUIT'S RING. A Romance of Mount Desert (12mo, paper, 50 cts.; cloth, $1.00).

"The conception of the story is excellent."— *The Boston Traveller.*

E. T. W. Hoffmann.

WEIRD TALES. With Portrait (12mo, 2 vols., $3.00).

"Hoffmann knew how to construct a ghost story quite as skilfully as Poe, and with a good deal more sense of reality. All those who are in search of a genuine literary sensation, or who care for the marvelous and supernatural, will find these two volumes fascinating reading."—*The Christian Union.*

Dr. J. G. Holland.

SEVEN OAKS—THE BAY PATH—ARTHUR BONNICASTLE—MISS GIL-BERT'S CAREER—NICHOLAS MINTURN.

Each, 12mo, $1.25; the set, $6.25.

"Dr. Holland will always find a congenial audience in the homes of culture and refinement. He does not affect the play of the darker and fiercer passions, but delights in the sweet images that cluster around the domestic hearth. He cherishes a strong fellow-feeling with the pure and tranquil life in the modest social circles of the American people, and has thus won his way to the companionship of many friendly hearts."—*The New York Tribune.*

Thomas A. Janvier.

COLOR STUDIES. (12mo, paper, 50 cts.; cloth, $1.00.)

"Piquant, novel, and ingenious, these little stories, with all their simplicity, have excited a wide interest. The best of them, 'Jaune D'Antimoine,' is a little wonder in its dramatic effect, its ingenious construction."—*The Critic.*

Virginia W. Johnson.

THE FAINALLS OF TIPTON. (12mo, $1.25.)

"The plot is good, and in its working-out original. Character-drawing is Miss Johnson's recognized *forte*, and her pen-sketches of the inventor, the checker-playing clergyman and druggist, the rising young doctor, the sentimental painter, the rival grocers, etc., are quite up to her best work."—*The Boston Commonwealth.*

Lieut. J. D. J. Kelley.

A DESPERATE CHANCE. (12mo, paper, 50 cts.; cloth, $1.00.)

"This novel is of the good old-fashioned, exciting kind. Though it is a sea story, all the action is not on board ship. There is a well-developed mystery, and while it is in no sense sensational, readers may be assured that they will not be tired out by analytical descriptions, nor will they find a dull page from first to last."—*The Brooklyn Union.*

The King's Men:

A TALE OF TO-MORROW. By Robert Grant, John Boyle O'Reilly, J. S. of Dale, and John T. Wheelwright. (12mo, $1.25.)

Andrew Lang.

THE MARK OF CAIN. (12mo, paper, 25 cts.)

"No one can deny that it is crammed as full of incident as it will hold, or that the elaborate plot is worked out with most ingenious perspicuity."—*The Saturday Review.*

George P. Lathrop.

NEWPORT. (12mo, paper, 50 cts.; cloth, $1.25)—**AN ECHO OF PASSION.** (12mo, paper, 50 cts.; cloth, $1.00)—**IN THE DISTANCE.** (12mo, paper, 50 cts.; cloth, $1.00.)

"It is one of the charms of Mr. Lathrop's style that it appeals to the imagination of the reader by a delicate suggestiveness, which lies like a fine atmosphere over the landscape of the story. His novels have the refinement of motive which characterize the analytical school, but his manner is far more direct and dramatic."—*The Christian Union.*

Brander Matthews.

THE SECRET OF THE SEA, and Other Stories. (12mo, paper, 50 cts.; cloth, $1.00)—**THE LAST MEETING.** (12mo, paper, 50 cts.; cloth, $1.00)— **IN PARTNERSHIP.** With H. C. Bunner (12mo, paper, 50 cts.; cloth, $1.00).

"Mr. Matthews is a man of wide observation and of much familiarity with the world. His literary style is bright and crisp, with a peculiar sparkle about it—wit and humor judiciously mingled— which renders his pages more than ordinarily interesting."—*The Rochester Post-Express.*

Fitz-James O'Brien.

THE DIAMOND LENS, with Other Stories. (12mo, paper, 50 cts.; cloth, $1.00.)

"These stories are the only things in literature to be compared with Poe's works, and if they do not equal it in workmanship, they certainly do not yield to it in originality."—*The Philadelphia Record.*

Duffield Osborne.

THE SPELL OF ASHTAROTH. (12mo, $1.00.)

Bliss Perry.

THE BROUGHTON HOUSE. (12mo, $1.25).

In this book Mr. Perry has presented an artistic and extraordinarily vivid picture of a New England town in summer, with close, shrewd, sympathetic, and wonderfully observant studies of its typical person-ages—the quartette of persons at the hotel, "The Broughton House," with whom the story is chiefly occupied, viewed against the background of the villagers and the natural environment.

Thomas Nelson Page.

IN OLE VIRGINIA—Marse Chan and Other Stories. (12mo, $1.25.)

"There are qualities in these stories of Mr. Page which we do not find in those of any other Southern author, or not to the same extent and in the same force—and they are the qualities which are too often wanting in modern literature."—*N, Y, Mail and Express.*

Saxe Holm's Stories.

FIRST SERIES.—Draxy Miller's Dowry—The Elder's Wife—Whose Wife Was She?—The One-Legged Dancers—How One Woman Kept Her Husband —Esther Wynn's Love Letters.

SECOND SERIES.—Four-Leaved Clover—Farmer Bassett's Romance—My Tourmalene—Joe Hale's Red Stocking—Susan Lawton's Escape.

Each, 12mo, paper, 50 cts.; cloth, $1.00.

"Saxe Holm's' characters are strongly drawn, and she goes right to the heart of human experience as one who knows the way. We heartily commend them as vigorous, wholesome, and sufficiently exciting stories."—*The Advance.*

Robert Louis Stevenson.

STRANGE CASE OF DR. JEKYLL AND MR. HYDE. (12mo, paper, 25 cts.; cloth, $1.00)—KIDNAPPED. (12mo, paper, 50 cts.; cloth, $1.00, illustrated, $1.25)—THE MERRY MEN, and Other Tales and Fables. (12mo, paper, 35 cts.; cloth, $1.00)—NEW ARABIAN NIGHTS. (12mo, paper, 30 cts.; cloth, $1.00)—THE DYNAMITER. With Mrs. Stevenson (12mo, paper, 30 cts.; cloth, $1.00)—THE BLACK ARROW. Illustrated (12mo, paper, 50 cts.; cloth, $1.00)—THE WRONG BOX. With Lloyd Osbourne (12mo, $1.00)—THE MASTER OF BALLANTRAE. A Winter's Tale. (12mo, paper, 50 cts.; cloth, illustrated, $1.25.)

"Stevenson belongs to the romantic school of fiction writers. He is original in style, charming, fascinating, and delicious, with a marvelous command of words, and with a manner ever delightful and magnetic. His style is as easy and as confidential as that of Defoe."—*The Boston Transcript.*

T. R. Sullivan.

DAY AND NIGHT STORIES. (12mo, Cloth, $1.00; Paper, 50 cents).— ROSES OF SHADOW. (12mo, $1.00).

"Mr. Sullivan's style is at once easy and refined, conveying most happily that atmosphere of good breeding and polite society which is indispensable to the novel of manners, but which so many of them lamentably fail of."—*The Nation.* "His style is clear and clean cut; his characters are genuine and observed."—*Saturday Review.*

Frederick J. Stimson (J. S., of Dale.)

GUERNDALE. (12mo, paper, 50 cts.; cloth, $1.25)—THE CRIME OF HENRY
VANE. (12mo, paper, 50 cts.; cloth, $1.00)—THE SENTIMENTAL CALEN-
DAR. Head Pieces by F. G. Attwood (12mo, $2.00)—FIRST HARVESTS.
An Episode in the Career of Mrs. Levison Gower, a Satire without a Moral
(12mo, $1.25)—THE RESIDUARY LEGATEE; or, The Posthumous Jest of
the Late John Austin. (12mo, paper, 35 cts.; cloth, $1.00.)

"No young novelist in this country seems better equipped than
Mr. Stimson is. He shows unusual gifts in this and in his other
stories."— *The Philadelphia Bulletin.*

Frank R. Stockton.

RUDDER GRANGE. (12mo, paper, 60 cts.; cloth, $1.25; illustrated by A. B.
Frost, Sq. 12mo, $2.00)—THE LATE MRS. NULL. (12mo, $1.25)—THE
LADY, OR THE TIGER? and Other Stories. (12mo, paper, 50 cts.; cloth,
$1.25)—THE CHRISTMAS WRECK, and Other Stories. (12mo, paper, 50
cts.; cloth, $1.25)—THE BEE-MAN OF ORN, and Other Fanciful Tales.
(12mo, cloth, $1.25)—AMOS KILBRIGHT, with Other Stories (12mo, paper,
50 cts.; cloth, $1.25).

The set, 6 vols., in a box, $7.50.

"Of Mr. Stockton's stories what is there to say, but that they
are an unmixed blessing and delight? He is surely one of the most
inventive of talents, discovering not only a new kind in humor and
fancy, but accumulating an inexhaustible wealth of details in each
fresh achievement, the least of which would be riches from another
hand."—W. D. HOWELLS, *in Harper's Magazine.*

Stories by American Authors.

Cloth, 16mo, 50c. each; set, 10 vols., $5.00; cabinet ed., in sets only, $7.50.

"The public ought to appreciate the value of this series, which
is preserving permanently in American literature short stories that
have contributed to its advancement. American writers lead all
others in this form of fiction, and their best work appears in these
volumes."— *The Boston Globe.*

John T. Wheelwright.

A CHILD OF THE CENTURY. (12mo, paper, 50 cts.; cloth, $1.00.)

"A typical story of political and social life, free from cynicism or
morbid realism, and brimming over with good-natured fun, which is
never vulgar."— *The Christian at Work.*